HOW TO MAKE MONSTERS

short stories by
Gary McMahon

Morrigan
books

www.morriganbooks.com

Published by Morrigan Books
Östra Promenaden 43
602 29 Norrköping
Sweden

www.morriganbooks.com

ISBN 978-91-977605-1-5

Cover art by Simon Strantzas ©2008

First Published September 2008
(previous publishing credits can be found on page 172)

ACKNOWLEDGEMENTS

Thanks go out to all the usual suspects — you know who you are; and if you don't, you're not one of them anyway. As always, love and big cuddles to my family.

This one is for Emily, who knows exactly how my monsters were made.

And for Joel Lane, whose support and enthusiasm have been invaluable.

"And that the lean abhorred monster keeps
Thee here in dark to be his paramour"

William Shakespeare, *Romeo and Juliet*,
Act 5 scene 3,

Cancer hag out on a date
Swinging on my garden gate
I'll kiss you as your face turns black
A show of love like an attack

Nefandor, *Croaker*
(Music and lyrics by Eddie and Eva Woe)

FOREWORD

Monsters. They are everywhere, all around.

Everywhere you look these days, there's one lounging against a car, smoking a cigarette, walking a dog, popping into the corner shop for a bottle of cheap cider, or voting at the local polling station on Election Day.

But where did they come from, these monsters? And why are they here?

The truth is that they've always been here: as long as man has walked the earth, our monsters have trailed in our wake, picking up our scraps and feeding off the carrion of our failures. In fact, just in case you haven't guessed yet, *we* are the monsters. We *are* them and we *made them*, creating their ragged forms from the meat of our regrets, filling their hot veins with the juice of our failed plans and dreams, giving them motion with the unrefined fuel of our memories.

Mary Shelley may have breathed life into the Modern Prometheus, but she wasn't the first; she was simply the first to write about the method employed to make her monster. The rest of us just carry on, trying to ignore the shambling figures; we attempt to outrun them by building lives, holding down jobs, having children, buying houses, driving cars, drinking fine wines and eating healthy food... but it won't work, not any of it. We can never be rid of the monsters we made; they are ours to own, and in turn they own us: it's a two-way street and there are no U-turns allowed.

We each make our own monster, and for every individual human being on the face of the earth there exists a different monster...

The rotten spirit of capitalism, the thing between the cracks, the ghosts of self, the school employees with terrible desires, debt, regret, racism, family ties, things that get in the way, our own faces, tradition, rejection, and the familiar shape of the darkness that lives deep inside our own hidden hearts.

I know exactly how I made my monsters, and day by day, bit by bit, I learn to live with them — even to take strength from them. How about you? Can you identify the component parts of your own monster, and can you afford the price you must pay for its construction?

Read on, and meet some people who couldn't.

Gary McMahon
2008
Leeds

CONTENTS

CHILL

Joel stood at the side of the motorway and looked for patterns in the hypnotic movement of the traffic. The sky above him was black and starless; the moon lurked behind a thick black sheet, afraid to show itself. The only light came from the car headlights and the tops of the concrete lamp posts standing like alien trees along the litter-strewn central reservation.

The somehow malleable sound of hot wheels on cold tarmac began to unnerve him, so he moved away, dragging his feet on the stubbly verge. An empty crisp packet, blown by the evening breeze, snatched at the cuffs of his trousers; he kicked it away, annoyed as if it were a living thing vying for his attention. Even inanimate objects, it seemed, would not leave him in peace.

The loud chirping of his mobile phone interrupted his thoughts. When he failed to answer it immediately, the impatient tone changed to a song or jingle he had no memory of programming into the handset.

He took the mobile from his coat pocket and raised it to his ear, placing it against the side of his head before pushing the right button — modern life, he knew, was all about pushing the right buttons.

"Hello." Traffic noise almost swallowed the word.

"Hi, Joel. It's me."

It took him a moment to place her voice. "Oh. Hi, Sue."

"Where are you? I've been waiting for you to come round. The heating's broken again. It's bloody cold. I could do with warming up."

Joel gritted his teeth. The simple declarative sentences she often used when she wanted something, her light manner, the sexual undertones in her soft voice: it all made him want to end the call, terminate the discussion before it had even begun. "I'm on my way," he said, glancing at the road, at the endless ribbon of traffic that promised an escape but never quite delivered. Where were they all going, these people? Everyone but him had a destination in mind, a route to follow.

"Joel?"

Sometimes he hated Sue. She could not understand his motivation for giving up a steady job with a reputable firm. His decision to leave the rat race had terrified her and she badgered him constantly to go back to work, to earn some decent money so he could buy the things everyone else did and fit into the narrow slot society had kept for him since birth.

Her limited view of the world sickened him, but not enough that he could give up the warmth of her body on a cold night, or the way she would happily fellate him almost on demand, even in a public place — *especially* in a public place.

"I'll be there in twenty minutes," he said, before tugging the phone away from his ear, drawing back his arm, and tossing the phone into the traffic. It clattered onto the hard road, spinning on some unknown axis until either a car or a small van rolled over it, smashing it to pieces and sending them skittering like insects.

"I don't want you!" he yelled, not knowing whether he meant the phone or the woman whose voice was barely contained within it. It didn't matter anyway, not now the thing was dead.

Joel walked away from the scene of his crime, following the line of the road as if it were a river that might lead to the open sea, feeling a sudden intense chill on his skin. The air had grown cold, and when he looked at the cars paused at the roundabout up ahead, he saw cobwebs of frost creeping across the rear windows.

If he cut across the wasteland to his left, then through the park, he could make it to Sue's house in less time than he'd promised. Climbing the low fence, he peered through the darkness; he could see the lights of her street from here, but they felt less than welcoming.

The traffic noise dimmed as he moved away from the road, walking carefully across the rocky ground towards the opposite fence, which ringed the council-owned play park. As he drew near, he began to pick out familiar shapes in the darkness: the immobile swings; the roundabout, moving gently in the wind; the monkey bars a seven year-old boy had been hanged from by a gang of teenagers only last summer. The boy had died slowly; his killers were still in youth custody and probably would be for years before they could be tried, sentenced, and finally — after serving shortened terms in a cushy jail — discreetly relocated abroad with new identities.

He climbed the other fence and entered the park. There was no one around: even the local kids were inside on a night as cold as this, or perhaps they kept away because of what had happened last summer, creating new myths and legends from the senseless murder of a small boy.

Stuffing his hands into his coat pockets, Joel stalked past the swings, not giving them as much as a glance. Something creaked — a dull, metallic sound — but he refused to acknowledge it and hurried his pace.

There was something on the slide: a long, humped shape perched at the bottom of the dimpled stainless steel ramp. Joel stopped, took his hands out of his pockets, and stared at the shape. It looked like a body, and for an instant he expected it to sit upright, its school clothes falling away to reveal a thin white neck with a knotted football scarf biting into the soft flesh.

The shape did not move. Was it a bundle of clothes dumped there by passing fly-tippers?

Joel took a step closer to the slide, his eyes watering, his throat dry. He looked behind him, at the distant lights of the motorway, and then back at the sight he knew he had to deal with.

The truth was obvious and inescapable. There was a body on the end of the slide.

He stared at it, not knowing what to do; unsure even if it was alive or dead. Reflexively, his hand went for his mobile phone, and he cursed himself for throwing it away. Why did he always have to act out of pique?

"Are you okay?" he took another step towards the body, hoping it was just a tramp sleeping off his nightly meths or cider intake. "Excuse me."

The body did not move. The ground beside was not littered with empty bottles, burned spoons, or used hypodermic syringes.

Joel put out a hand, left it there, hovering only inches away from the body. It looked like a man, but it was difficult to be sure. He was wrapped up in rags, and there were what looked like used bank notes stuck to his frost-coated clothing. Bills and receipts clung to his dark scalp and the flaky remains of his face. Joel tried not to stare at the decayed features, but was unable to look away from a mouth that yawned far too wide beneath a flattened nose, and eye sockets so deformed that they were beginning to meet in the middle of the misshapen head.

Vomit rose in his throat and he was at last able to avert his gaze. He ran across the park, heading in the direction of Sue's street, where the lights still burned brightly. Once there, he could use her land line to call the police. His feet caught on tufts of frosted grass; his breath misted before his eyes, making it difficult to see. The night seemed darker than before.

"Keep going," he muttered through lips cold and sticky as ice cream. "*Just go.*"

He followed the crude, unmade pathway that rose from the main park area and terminated near the end of Sue's street. His feet slipped on loose stones but he did not fall. The undergrowth rustled as something darted behind a bush, but he tried not to allow the sudden commotion to divert his attention. The air closed in on him, wrapping chilled fingers around his arms and shoulders. He shrugged off the cold, thinking instead of the warmth of Sue's flesh, the moist cavern of her open mouth.

Slowing now, he spotted a motionless couple at the head of the path, leaning against the broad metal post which served as a demarcation point between waste ground and residential street, a loosely defined line between the two extremes of wildness and urbanity. The couple were locked in an intimate embrace. They did not move, simply stood there, mouth-to-mouth, skin-to-skin, heart-to-heart. Their hands clasped each other's clothing with a desperation Joel found nauseating.

"Excuse me," said Joel as he squeezed by. "I need to call the police."

There was no response; the couple were frozen in place, locked in an embrace that even time might not break. The cold rose from their bodies as a vapour, coiling like pale smoke from an unseen fire.

Joel ran along the street, heading for Sue's house. Once there, this nightmare could end; a sense of reality would surely slot back into place around him. A group of youths in tracksuits stood outside one of the few darkened houses on the street, hoodies pulled up to cover their heads, stark white faces peering out with frozen expressions of loss and confusion. At their feet, a small dog was frozen to a garden wall, caught in the act of urinating, one leg extended, the paw adhered to the shiny brickwork.

The youths turned slowly in Joel's direction; their movements were stiff, graceless, and even their eyes were glazed over with a skein of white frost.

As he ran, Joel became aware of the slowing movement of the planet beneath him, the grinding down of the heavens above. Everything was sticking in place, becoming rigid; society's mechanisms were seizing up, the whole falling apart: the centre would not hold, not now. Too many things had changed; too much horror had been let loose by those who sought only to control the forces they had created. The war in Iraq… the U.S. credit crunch… the looming oft-promised crash of the property market. All the world's systems were failing, freezing; there were cold days and harsh nights ahead, and Joel no longer felt part of the plan.

Sue wanted to marry him when her divorce finally came through, but all Joel wanted was to lose himself in the crowd, to become less than a number on whatever computer hard drive stored the information — names, dates, and statistics — of the populace. Their relationship was like a corpse he'd been carrying on his back, dragging it around for so long that he had grown accustomed to its rotting weight. But now, in the middle of this current crisis, it was all he had left to cling to.

He threw himself against Sue's front door, only noticing the iced-over windows when he paused for breath.

"Let me in!" He hammered on the door with hands gone numb from the cold. "Please... *Sue!*"

Staring at the front window, trying to see inside through the glazed patterns on the glass, he was certain that a figure stood unmoving at the window, a hand raised to its mouth. Frozen in place, like a waxwork dummy or a snapshot of how things used to be, were meant to be, before the big freeze set in.

He turned around and stumbled back down the path. The kids on the corner were still there, but incapable of even the most rudimentary movements. One of them went down, falling against the kerb, short torso shattering into large chunks that lay in the gutter like discarded meat products from a bankrupt freezer shop.

Joel stopped dead in his tracks, stunned into immobility.

The man from the slide was standing near the gate next door, staring in Joel's direction; the partial face was, thankfully, obscured by the flapping paper receipts, torn and creased official forms and bus tickets that served as a cobbled-together mask.

"*Follow me.*" The voice was like stones rolling loose in a plastic bowl.

"*Follow. Me.*"

Joel began to cry but the tears froze on his cheeks. He stared down at his hands, his small white hands, and when he tried to open them the fingers snapped, one of them breaking off and falling to the ground between his feet. There was no pain; all feeling had gone. The chill had numbed him.

"*Follow.*" There were other hazy figures behind this one, others who had chosen to make the transition and be saved. Sue was lost to him now, along with everything she represented. His old dreams were frozen, and to wake from them he must do as the figure commanded.

Joel stepped forward on legs growing stiffer, weaker, and more unresponsive with each passing second, and followed the man into a chilled, white world where something different — perhaps even another, better way of living — was preparing to hatch out of the ice.

THROUGH THE CRACKS

There was a crack in the train window. Emma stared at the fine imperfection, imagining that in a sudden wind the crack would open and everyone inside the speeding vehicle would be sucked out and killed on the tracks. Or perhaps when the train thundered through an underground tunnel, something older than the railways would crawl inside through the crack; summoned by the flickering electric lights, the smell of human sweat and the low sound of murmured conversations, it would feast upon the commuters.

When her mobile phone began to vibrate, signalling an incoming call, Emma suddenly forgot where and when she was; her mind had drifted to a time many years ago, when such cracks had threatened to appear in the substance of reality all because of the insanity of one man — a man whose name and face she could never forget.

She had not spoken to Prentiss in three years, so when his name appeared on the screen on the front of the phone, accompanied by a shrill version of some forgettable chart hit, Emma's initial instinct was to hang up without speaking. But she didn't; instead she calmly watched the blocky text flashing on the small rectangular screen, wondering what he could want, and why she'd left his details in the gadget's memory anyway.

"Hello," she finally answered, holding the handset tight against her ear to minimise the noise of the train as it hurtled over uneven tracks towards Newcastle. "Hello. Prent, is that you?"

Nothing. Not even the familiar whispery hiss of static. Just a long, almost baleful silence on the other end of the line. Then she heard a sound like glass or crockery breaking; a loud crunching crackle that made her pull her hand away from the side of her head and screw up her face in an expression of distaste. Was he toying with her, testing what reaction he might receive after all this time?

"*Hello*," she said, loudly, one more time, finger hovering over the green hang-up button.

"*Em?* Emma, it's me. It's Prentiss." His voice was faint, as if coming to her across a vast distance. Then there was a surge in volume and she could hear him more clearly. "How are you?"

"Hi, Prent. I'm good. Long time no hear." It was typical of him to call her up out of the blue, as if nothing had happened between them. That complete disregard for the social rituals had been part of why they'd split up in the first place. That and about a million other things: half-hidden cracks in his personality that had become all-too apparent during their time together.

"I've been thinking about you." The statement sent a faint chill of anticipation along her nerve endings, culminating between her legs. No matter how weird Prentiss had become, how strange his behaviour had been, Emma had long ago resigned herself to the fact that she would always be attracted to him.

"Oh." The train went under a tunnel; the connection broke for a few seconds so she could not be completely sure of what he said next.

"—so I've been a bit low lately. Things have been strange." What had she missed? It seemed important, but she didn't want to ask him to repeat whatever he'd said; her feelings were always so damn messy when it came to dealing with Prentiss that she was unable to act in anything approaching a normal, rational manner.

"Can I see you?"

"I live in London now, Prent. I left the north east eighteen months ago."

"Really? Well that one took me by surprise."

"I'm visiting my sister this weekend." She regretted telling him this as soon as the words passed her lips. "I guess I could meet you somewhere."

"It's like fate, isn't it?"

Emma did not reply.

"I'm having… *difficulty* leaving the house. Could you come round? I'm still living in the same place."

"Yes. Okay. Tomorrow evening." She hung up before she could even question her response. The train carried her towards home, and towards yet another ill thought out meeting with her ex. As bright winter sunlight battered her with harsh lightning strokes through the long carriage windows, Emma wondered why, wherever Prentiss was concerned, she could never bring herself to say no.

She arrived in Central Station just after midday, and dodged the bustling December crowds to catch a Metro to her sister's place out near the airport. Yet another capsule rocketing through underground caverns; somehow this seemed like a metaphor for a part of her life she'd tried so very hard to leave behind. The stations flew by in a blur. Monument. Haymarket. Jesmond (rendered dark with memories of Prentiss). Ilford Road. Place names rendered meaningless because of her relocation to the Smoke. A group of youths in regulation white tracksuits got on at South Gosforth, the only feature distinguishing one from the next being the colour and brand of their baseball caps. The boys — aged between fourteen and sixteen — lounged with their feet up on the seats and drank cheap cider from dented cans; Emma felt relieved to be getting off the train at the next stop.

Nicci's house was a five minute walk from the station, past tired looking shop fronts with dusty window displays consisting of canned and boxed goods Emma hadn't seen advertised in over ten years. Steel bars and vandal-proof glass marked the way; the sacred landscape of her youth was deteriorating a little more each day she stayed away. Certain parts of the footpaths seemed cracked beyond repair, big gaping fissures opening up in the grubby concrete paving slabs to reveal the dark grasping earth beneath.

Emma hurried towards Nicci's house, and when she approached the door it was opened without her having to announce her arrival.

"Em! Welcome home!" Her sister's chunky arms went around her, and she was bustled inside and into the warm environment. Food smells accosted her nostrils; the sound of a radio greeted her from another room. This was better. This was more like home.

They chatted over coffee and biscuits, Emma trying not to comment on Nicci's recent weight gain. It seemed that her sister's husband had started a new job, long-distance lorry driving between the UK and Germany. Ed was away for long stints, but according to Nicci this made the time he spent at home with her and the kids all the more worthwhile.

Emma's nephews, Olly and Jared, were over at a friend's house for some pre-teenaged birthday party, and would return much later, stuffed to idleness with the unhealthy delights of chocolate and cake. Emma was glad of the time alone with her sister; quiet moments like these happened all too rarely these days, and their intimacy helped remind her that she hadn't just left the bad things behind.

"Mum and dad send their love," Nicci said, smiling broadly. "I got an email last night."

"I've been a bit lazy in contacting them. My computer crashed a few weeks ago, and I seem to have forgotten how to use the phone..."

Nicci grinned, appreciating that Emma had never been a strong communicator, and that she'd never approved of their parents' emigration, designed so that they could spend their retirement in the sun. "It's expensive to call Australia," she said, reaching out across the table to brush Emma's hand in a rare show of solidarity. "I'm sure they understand."

The rest of the afternoon passed quickly, and all too soon the kids arrived back from the party. Olly was unable to hide his affection for his aunt, and smothered her with rich candy-flavoured kisses; Jared was more insular, and merely pecked at her offered cheek before slouching off to the bathroom to get ready for bed.

The travelling had tired Emma more than she cared to admit, and when she started to doze in front of the television Nicci ordered her up to bed. "You're in the spare room, the one next to the boys' room. I've put fresh sheets on the bed, and there's a stereo set up in there in case you want to listen to some music before turning in."

Emma hugged her sister hard, afraid that if she let go this moment might shatter like glass. When Nicci broke free, a look of amused concern on her face, Emma shook her head and trotted silently upstairs.

Sleep teased her mercilessly, staying just out of reach, jerking away from her mind whenever she got close enough to grab its tenuous, mist-like essence. She thought of Prentiss, and of his obsessions. The way he'd become convinced that reality was shredding like old wallpaper in a derelict house and something nasty was peering through from the other side.

It was these frightening notions that had finally led to the breakdown of affection between them; Emma had loved him right up until the end, but had eventually been forced to admit that sometimes love isn't enough. He refused to seek professional help, remaining convinced that he was sane and stable, despite the protestations of the few friends he had left. When Emma had walked away for the last time, Prentiss had been too afraid of his own phantoms to even follow her out the door.

And now, three years later, did the same madness still drive him? Was he still seeing demons, or had he rid himself of the fantasy life that had driven a wedge between them?

Finally, she slept, but dark smudges stained her dreams, shapeless fractures that gaped in the corners of her imagination, put there by Prentiss too long ago to trouble her waking mind.

ം

"For God's sake, Em, don't tell me you're going to see him?" Nicci's face was contorted into a snarl; she couldn't mention Prentiss' name without it scarring her features. "The bloke's a psycho. Didn't he run off chasing monsters, or something?"

"No," Emma replied, placing her teacup on a floral-patterned coaster. "He locked himself away so that they couldn't get him."

"Oh, well excuse my mistake. That makes a *big* difference." Nicci stood and walked to the window, looking out at her boys playing football in the huge back garden. A smile played across her face at the sight, but then she remembered that she was supposed to be angry. Emma loved her unquestionably in that moment, gaining a glimpse into the heart of motherhood; a peek at a state of mind that she someday dearly wished to experience for herself.

"He sounded rational, Nic. Like he's got himself together."

Her sister turned away from the window, an apple tree framing her, giving the illusion of devil horns sticking out the sides of her head. "You always went back to him," she said, the anger having fled in the face of genuine concern. "And he always exploited that."

"Things are different now. I have my own life, a new start. I'm strong now; I don't need him to lean on."

"No," said her sister. "You have that all wrong. It was always him who leaned on you."

The taxi arrived at 6:30, and Nicci walked her to the door. "Be careful," she said, tenderly. "Don't let him use you again."

Emma kissed Nicci's cheek and climbed into the cab, watching the suburban view unfurl as they neared the outskirts of the city. Prentiss lived in a shared house in Jesmond, a huge Victorian terraced property with rooms so big each one could have contained her entire flat in Bermondsey with enough space left over to squeeze in a single bed.

All too soon the ride was over, and Emma paid the driver and watched him pull away from the kerb. Trees lined the verges, their branches bare; some of them bore splits in their wide flaking trunks, possibly the result of some kind of elm disease. The footpaths here were in better condition than the ones in Nicci's neighbourhood, but still the area seemed to be falling slowly into ruin. Gardens were overgrown; the brickwork of some of the houses was badly in need of repair; even the sky looked broken, shattered into giant slivers, like a damaged picture window.

She could remember the place is if she'd visited it only yesterday. Surely Prentiss's housemates would have changed a few times by now, but she knew his room would look exactly the same. The last time she'd been inside, there had been newspaper clippings stuck to the walls, stories about environmental disasters, nuclear meltdowns, landmark buildings crumbling into dereliction. Prentiss's obsession with social decay had been only the start of it; from there, his preoccupations had taken a darker turn. When the books about atrocities had turned up on his shelves, Emma had finally spoken out and begged him to talk to a doctor. It wasn't natural, she claimed, to read constantly about the Holocaust, Bosnian war crimes, the hell of WW1 trenches.

Prentiss had explained it all away by saying that modern society needed to embrace the darkness at its core, if only to prevent that darkness from taking hold of us all over again, to stop it reaching through the gaps to pull us down.

Thinking about all of this, Emma almost walked away. Her hand hovered over the doorbell, and she conducted an interior argument with herself as to whether or not she should return to Nicci's and order a Chinese takeaway.

The door opened; a figure stood well back from the threshold, visible only as shadow, and beckoned her inside. "Hurry," said the shadow. "Come on in."

It was Prentiss. He'd been waiting for her.

"I thought you might not come," he said as she followed him along a damp, badly decorated hallway. The stairs creaked ominously as they climbed to his room, but Emma was beyond being nervous under such conditions. Prentiss was a shred of the man he'd used to be. His clothes hung on him like rags, his hair was thinning at the scalp, and his skin had taken on a sickly yellow sheen. He looked ill, and Emma knew that if things got out of hand she could easily send him to the floor with a well-placed right-hook.

"I thought you might be... better," she said, following him into his room, the interior of which proved her prognosis to be utterly without foundation.

Prentiss sat on the bed, clearing a space with his hand. Papers scattered to the floor, but he made no move to pick them up. Emma could see they were covered in scrawled notes, unintelligible hand-written theories that still had a grip on his mind.

"Thank you for coming," he said, smiling nervously. As he was now, Emma had great difficulty understanding exactly what it was about him that had attracted her in the first place. He was a shell, a self-abused puppet flopping on severed strings.

Suddenly she became aware of the smell: a damp, flat odour that was difficult to place. Then, when she saw the state of what parts of the walls and ceiling remained visible, she realised what it was. Wet plaster. Opened plastic pots of Polyfilla repair paste and crack sealant sat on the windowsill, battered cutlery sticking up out of the white doughy mass within.

Prentiss had been filling cracks. The stuff hung in abstract stalactites from the ceiling, in frozen drips down the walls. Any crack — however superficial — had been stuffed and inexpertly covered with the malleable material.

If it were not for his debauched and denuded appearance, Emma would have fled. But even now, in this vastly reduced state, he still retained a magnetic pull on her emotions. She gravitated towards him, even though the stench of urine and halitosis that rose from him in a cloud made her want to back away. He cut a pathetic figure in his stained T Shirt and ripped black jeans; his torso flashed white and spare under the baggy clothing. Emma had never seen him so thin. He looked positively malnourished.

"Why did you ask me here?" She thought a direct approach might at least yield one or two vaguely coherent answers.

Prentiss stood up from the mattress, a hand going up under his shirt to scratch a dry sore on his concave belly. Emma drew in a breath; as he turned, she could clearly define his ribs and the vicious ripple of spine through the scant covering of skin and atrophied muscle. Prentiss, she realised, was visibly wasting away.

"One of my housemates knows your sister — he drinks in the pub where she sometimes does shifts behind the bar. I knew you were coming, Emma... I'm sorry. I needed to talk to someone, and you were the only one who ever believed me. The only one who *listened*."

"I never believed you." The truth was her only recourse now; Prentiss had been fooling himself for too long and she no longer wanted to be complicit in the deception. "All I ever did was humour you. And when you didn't get the message, I left."

His smile was grim, like a widening crack that slowly crawled over the lower part of his waxy face. Emma had the insane urge to plug it with sealant from the tubs lined up on the floor by the end of the bed.

"I see," he said, sitting back down and rubbing the side of his head with an open palm, wincing as something — some undefined pain — bothered him. "I understand."

"You need help, Prent. You've needed it for a long time."

"Nobody can help me." His face softened, becoming both more and less than the sharp angles of his bone structure. It was as if a form more solid than his features could hint at was trying to push through from inside his skull. "I've spent all these years looking for them, examining the gaps, and now that they're finally here no one believes me.

"They're coming, Emma. *Coming through the cracks.*"

Emma suddenly felt very afraid, not only for her own physical wellbeing, but also for her old boyfriend's sanity. This was real madness, close to the bone and way out over the edge. Prentiss had completely lost his mind.

"I'm going now," she mumbled, slipping her hands into her pockets and trying to act like this situation was the most normal thing in the world. "I have to get back — Nicci will be wondering where I am."

26

Prentiss said nothing; just stared at a spot on the floor, eyes wide and seeing beyond the worn weave of the carpet.

Emma opened the door and glanced back over her shoulder. Prentiss was now on his feet, moving slowly towards her, a large scrapbook held out like an offering. "Take it," he said. "Please. Just take it and read what's inside."

She turned to face him and took the book, smiling coldly as she stepped backwards through the door and out onto the landing. The door closed in her face; Prentiss did not pursue her out of the strange world that was his grubby double room. She took the stairs two at a time, forgetting about the book in her hand. Once out on the street, she ran towards the nearest Metro station, jumping the cracks in the pavement and praying that she would not have to wait long for a train.

At some point during the journey, she remembered that she was holding the scrapbook. Carefully, as if she were handling some extremely fragile artefact, she opened the book. The pages were stained and dog-eared from overuse, and the narrow spine was torn. Inside were pasted articles from obscure periodicals, smudged prints of digital images downloaded from amateur fortean websites, and yet more hand-written notes.

Emma scanned a few of the articles, her blood seeming to thicken in her arteries.

A report of a Djinn terrorising a cave network somewhere in the desert outside Dubai in the United Arab Emirates; the caves were fed by underground streams which were part of some immense subterranean network of gulfs and chasms: cracks in the belly of the earth.

An earthquake in Argentina, and the subsequent sightings of a strange spider-limbed demon prowling in the foothills of some local mountains.

Cave divers reported missing in the Yorkshire Dales.

Babies stolen from a hospital in Mexico, whose basement was recently damaged in a terrorist bomb blast, the foundations splitting open to reveal a deep underground crevasse.

They were coming. Coming through the cracks.

Emma shook her head, trying to dislodge Prentiss's crazy statement. This was not evidence; it was merely random information used to support his own delusion, a framework upon which he could hang his fantasies. You could prove anything to yourself if you were desperate enough, even this utter nonsense.

When she eventually made it back to Nicci's place, Emma remained withdrawn and pensive until it was time for her nephews to go to bed. Then she read them a bedtime story before soaking in a hot bath. She lay in the steaming tub with her eyes open, staring at the ceiling. There was a crack above the toilet she'd not noticed the day before.

Her aimless dozing was interrupted by a knock on the door; Nicci's voice drifted in to break her reverie: "Em, you okay? Can I come in?"

"No, I'm fine. Really. Just a bit down after seeing Prentiss. But you can rest easy. It's over. I won't be seeing him again."

"Okay, hon. I'm here to talk if you need me."

Emma glanced over at the scrapbook she'd balanced on the rim of the sink. She almost called Nicci back, asked her to look at what was inside the tatty covers. But no, to do so would have felt too much like willingly entering Prentiss's nightmares. The only cracks she knew of where the ones in his sanity.

Bath time over, she dried herself off and went to bed, looking forward to the end of her stay. She was due to return to London the next day and any enjoyment she'd taken from the trip had been tarnished by her communication with Prentiss. Even now, he was able to ruin small parts of her life, and she resented the power he had over her.

"I'll miss you," said Nicci, holding her tight on the doorstep. "Come back soon, big sis."

Emma returned the hug, and wished that she felt more like staying; it would cost her nothing to extend her trip, to spend more quality time with her family, but right now the thought of leaving Prentiss's ever-widening circle of influence seemed like a very good idea. "I'll be back at Christmas," she said. "In three weeks time. I promise."

Olly and Jared followed her outside, trailing her along the street as she headed for the Metro. They were good boys, full of life and energy, and she brushed away a tear as they ran off towards the park, waving and calling her name. Even Jared had seemed sad to see her go.

The next train was delayed by ten minutes, and Emma felt herself drawn to her mobile phone. She took it out of her pocket, dialled Prentiss's number, but didn't press the button to connect the call. She repeated this procedure three more times before finally giving in to temptation.

The phone rang out at the other end; no one was home.

Feeling deeply uneasy, Emma checked her watch. The London train wasn't scheduled to leave Newcastle until three o'clock. It was just after one. If she was quick, she could call in on him, just to check that he hadn't done anything foolish.

The train arrived. She got on, knowing exactly at which station she'd disembark.

She made it to the house in plenty of time, telling herself that all she was planning to do was check on Prentiss' wellbeing. If he'd had an accident, or even tried to kill himself, she would never be able to look at herself in the mirror again. Despising her own weakness, and his passive strength, she rang the doorbell.

The door opened and a stranger stepped outside. "Oh, hi," he said, pulling a woollen hat down over his shaven head. "You here to visit someone?"

"Yes, Prentiss O'Neil." She realised this must be one of the people he shared the house with.

"Ah. I think the queer bugger's still in his room. I haven't seen him for days. If he is in, tell him he owes me fifty quid for the gas bill, would you." Then he was gone, jogging along the street towards the bus stop that was located outside a tiny video rental shop that seemed only to stock titles from the 1980s.

Emma pushed open the door and went inside, wiping her feet on the threadbare doormat. The house was silent; a stale heaviness hung in the air. She climbed the stairs to Prentiss' first floor room and knocked on his door, her touch lighter than intended. When no answer came, she knocked again, louder this time. The door swung open under the increased pressure from her knuckles.

Emma took a step inside, smelling that same dry yet moist odour and sensing that something was very wrong. The room was dark, the blinds pulled over the single window, and looked in even worse disarray than during her last visit.

"Prent. You here?" She expected no reply, and none came.

There was a naked figure kneeling on the bed, turned to face the wall. It was male — she could at least make out that pertinent detail in the gloom — and his hands were flattened against the peeling wallpaper. Drawing closer, she noticed that the floor was covered in a layer of crumbled plaster; the cracks Prentiss had crudely attempted to repair had opened up, shedding their DIY skin.

"Prent?" She could tell it was him from the familiar curvature of his spine, and the small tattoo of a Rose on his left shoulder.

"What the hell—"

She stopped in the centre of the room, poised to take another step but not quite managing it.

From this angle it looked as if he had tried to force his head into the long diagonal crack in the wall that ran in a jagged line from the corner of the window frame. She could see the soles of his feet on the bed, his legs, taut and skinny, his pallid back, his neck... but nothing above that.

Then, with growing horror, she realised her mistake.

Prentiss had not stuck his head into the crack; the crack had spread across the wall, passing through flesh and bone to shear off most of his head above the jaw line. Prentiss' skull had become part of the fracture, a jagged black rent through which only darkness could be viewed.

As Emma watched, the wall around the crack seemed to shiver and the area of damage widened. Its messy Rosarch edges sent out spidery limbs to breach plasterboard and brickwork and splinter the dead matter of Prentiss' rigid torso.

The crack was growing; something was trying to climb out.

Emma ran from the room, slamming the door to shut the

monstrosity inside. She stumbled to the station and jumped on the first train to arrive, heading into the heart of the city. Perhaps safety lay in numbers, surrounded by crowds. But there were cracks everywhere: cracks in buildings, in road surfaces, even in people.

When she reached the station she sat in a glassed-walled waiting room under a row of stark fluorescent bulbs. At least where there was too much light she would see them coming, be alerted to their presence before they reached her. She pulled up her feet onto the bench, listening to the groan of plastic, hoping that it would not break. Or crack.

THE UNSEEN

For Mark Lynch

(What follows is the slightly edited version of a hand-written manuscript found in July 2005, wrapped in an old cellophane sandwich bag and wedged into a hole in the wall of a derelict house in the West End of Newcastle upon Tyne. The sheets were undated, and no author's name was legible.)

Our numbers are many, yet still we remain unseen, unnoticed; the vast majority of you honest, law-abiding citizens walk past us on the city streets every day, not even realising that we are there. We are the forgotten. The cast-offs. The outsiders.

We are those who observe you as you go about your business.

Utilising this questionable advantage bestowed upon us by our low social standing, we watch. And what we see is sometimes incredible.

I've always kept notebooks, and now that for some reason I've been chosen to chronicle the inexplicable, the stark and sometimes depressing truth of our busy little peaceable kingdoms, I have taken care to maintain the habit. Back in my old life, I was a writer of fictions: I wrote thrillers and detective stories, fooling myself into believing that they mattered, and eking out a modest existence from the words I produced. These days the mysteries are real, but my style of recording them has not changed. I have no publisher, no agent, no means of getting my work "out there", but these things are no longer important to me. All that matters is getting it all down on paper.

I keep a locker in Central Station, and fill it with my loose pages and messy notebooks (no doubt this document will end up there too, taking up space with the rest). Some day they will be important, these seemingly random scribblings penned by a man on the edge; until then they sit, dusty and neglected, waiting for their time to come.

I'm not quite sure when I first saw them, but I do know when I first noticed their existence. It was Friday evening, a boom time for we who live on the streets: drunken celebrants will put their hand in their pockets to impress their dates; pissed-up workers letting off steam might buy you a kebab or a burger from one of the countless fast food outlets down by the Bigg Market.

I was lounging by Grey's Monument with my close pal The Spiker. We were sharing a bottle of rum he'd managed to lift from an off-license in the Cattle Market, and indulging our usual habit of people-watching. It's what we do; all we have. When you're down on your luck, you tend to become very observant. You notice a pound coin dropped by a rushing commuter, a half-eaten packet of crisps thrown into a litter bin at a bus stop, the way some people will announce that they're a soft touch purely by the slant of their mouth or a soft, vague light in their eyes.

The sun was just setting, dragging crimson-hued acid trails through an unusually low and heavy sky resigned to dull grey for most of the day. The Spiker went quiet — he's usually an incessant talker — and we both just watched for a while, content to pass the bottle between us in an easy, companionable silence.

And that was when I saw it, out of the corner of my eye. Later, I began to realise that was the only way to see them: peripheral. If you look dead-on, you won't see a thing.

A visibly stressed young mother was bending down to chastise her baby outside a betting shop, her tired face lurid and mask-like in the lowering light. The baby was having a tantrum over some silly incident that matters only to the very young, and the woman was obviously at the end of her tether.

As she bent to the pushchair, delivering a rapid open-handed slap to the side of the child's head and screaming some indecipherable obscenity, a shadow crossed between her and the subject of her disapproval. It was like a ripple in the air, a slight distortion in one of reality's layers.

And then it was gone. The woman pushed the baby out into the main flow of foot traffic, becoming lost in the crowd, and I was left feeling puzzled. Surely I couldn't have seen what I thought I had: the vague rumour of a face hovering in the air.

The Spiker and I got roaring drunk that night, so I gave no further thought to the event. We snagged a couple of bottles of Thunderbird from a bunch of students on a night out to celebrate passing their exams, and retreated to a local squat we knew to pass the time.

At 5 am I found myself flat on my back and wrapped up in a stinking sheet next to some woman whose body I couldn't recall having lain beside. Her hair was thick with dirt, and I could barely make out her face through the layer of soot that seemed to have accumulated there for some reason. I sincerely doubted that anything physical had occurred; I had been unable to sustain an erection for over a year.

Stiff, tired and hung-over, I got up and walked outside to swallow some fresh air.

We were up on the first floor of an old condemned office complex on Pink Lane, were the whores and junkies gather, and I stood on the fire escape and spied on the sleeping city below. Early risers — Worm-catchers, as we called them — tramped the slumbering streets leading from the train station, heading for early shifts, returning from all-night parties, or just trying to walk the night out of their system.

Through the hazy morning air I thought that I could see misty shadows hanging from them, like the remnants of bad dreams. It was an odd sight, lonely and rather frightening, but I put it down to the cheap booze and began to climb down the folding metal ladder to the street below.

Finding some loose change in my pocket, I went into a McDonald's for a coffee. It was the only place willing to open that early, and I regretted spending the cash, but I had nowhere else to go, nobody to see. Time alone was what I needed, if only to clear my throbbing head.

After the coffee, I walked the streets, waiting for the people to arrive. Saturday morning shoppers were never generous, but sometimes patience might be rewarded with a few quid thrown at you by some witless wag who thought it was the epitome of humour to piss on you from a great height when you were down on your knees. I didn't mind: money is money, no matter the manner in which it is given.

I walked, sat in shop doorways and avoided company. A few other faces I knew were patrolling their habitual spots, but all they got from me was a nod of the head, a wink of the eye. I was in no mood for chat.

Some time around 10 am, I saw my ex wife. She was alone, climbing out of a taxi on High Bridge Street. There were a few fancy boutiques in that area, and I guessed that she was shopping for some new clothes to replace last season's wardrobe.

I felt nothing when I saw her. The hate had gone long ago, replaced now by a sort of bitter acceptance. I meant her no harm, not any more. Attacking her that one time had cleared my system of the need to hurt, and now all I wanted was to get on with whatever flyblown tatters of a life I had left.

When my book sales had dried up, she'd left me to move in with my accountant. The two of them had fleeced me for what little savings I had, leaving me without a bean to my name. She even took the house in the divorce, which left me homeless. The drinking soon followed, and before I knew it the world had skidded out from under me and I was living in a corrugated steel garden shed out near Four Lane Ends.

We are all just a short step from the gutter, and if someone chooses to nudge us in the wrong direction, we can fall in without making as much as a splash.

I don't hate my wife. I pity her. She became addicted to the trappings of being married to a local minor celebrity — the clothes, the parties, the flash cars — and when it all went away she'd forgotten why we'd fallen in love in the first place.

I ducked behind a wall, ensuring that she wouldn't see me, and in my haste I managed to turn my ankle on the kerb. Sitting down heavily on the pavement, I massaged the area, hoping that I hadn't broken a bone. People like me have no doctor we can go and see, and we are treated like garbage if we go to the hospital casualty ward. Having no social security number, and no valid ID, we are nothing, ghosts. Such is the price of dropping out.

Feeling a slight but persistent need to be underground, I made for the nearest Metro entrance and hobbled down the stairs. There was a train due in three minutes, so I stood and ignored the dirty looks and muttered comments until it arrived in a screech of air brakes through the huge black oval of the tunnel.

If you jump the barrier at the right station, and keep your eyes open while you ride the trains, you can spend a couple of hours down there in the cool darkness before some overzealous prick of a conductor throws you off the system for not having a ticket.

As I made my way along the train, shambling from carriage to carriage, I saw people glance away if I caught their gaze. They thought I was begging, and the rationale in such situations is that if you ignore the annoyance it will go away. It's an attitude that's always amused me, but lately it had begun to provoke only fear and a mute form of rage.

I saw The Spiker sitting alone in the carriage nearest the driver. He waved at me as I approached, and I dragged myself along the greasy handrails to join him.

"You okay, mate?" he asked, nodding at my leg.

"Aye, fell over that's all. Still a bit muggy from last night."

He let out a baying donkey laugh. "Not surprised," he said. "Especially after bedding down with Scary Mary!"

I sighed, realising that I really should have recognised the woman I'd woken up next to. Scary Mary: a petite middle-aged Scottish woman who'd been fleeing an abusive husband for the past eighteen months. Her fits of temper were legendary, and I'd probably upset her by doing a vanishing act.

"What you up to, then?" I asked, trying to divert my friend's attention from last night's transgression.

"Not much," he said. "You want one of these?"

He produced a couple of rigid iced buns from the folds of his thin coat, leaving a layer of sugar in the lining. Back in his old life, when he had a job and a mainstream routine, The Spiker had used to date a girl who worked at Starbucks. She'd kept up the acquaintance, sneaking him food whenever she could — usually day-old sandwiches and stale pastries; stuff meant for the waste bin — and he always shared his haul with me. That's how we operated: as a loose team, dividing to conquer the gnawing pangs of hunger.

It was right about then, when I was sitting munching on a confectionary in the shadow-striped quiet as we journeyed under the city, that I became aware of faint movement around me in the carriage. It was as if the other passengers began to twitch when I wasn't looking, and whenever I turned to see they stopped moving.

I stared at my hands, counting the crumbs on my fingers as I chewed the last of the food. And saw it at the edges of my vision: fast, blurred movement, like something that shifted quicker than the eye darting only partially into view.

Faces. Hands. Open mouths. The glimmering shapes of unusually supple bodies as they disturbed the still, stale air. Each passenger had a sketchy double, a barely-glimpsed twin, and these *others* were hanging from them like unruly children, grasping, silently pleading.

I kept staring at my hands, the big, scarred knuckles, wondering if I was going insane.

There was one sitting on The Spiker's knee, holding his head in its hands and silently screaming into his face. But he was completely unaware, blind to its presence.

When I looked directly at him, it was gone.

Then the train pulled squealing into a station, and I hobbled out onto the crowded platform, pushing my way through weekend shoppers and dazed tourists. I could hear the Spiker calling my name, but I ignored him, not wanting to see that thing on him ever again.

I'm not sure how long I kept running (or limping), only that it didn't seem to be an escape from what I'd seen. They were everywhere, those things: holding people's hands as they strolled beneath a weak and heartless sun, sitting across from lovers in bars and cafes, squatting morosely in the back seats of cars. Some of them were quite well defined, and the same size as the people they were dogging; but others were small and withered, emaciated effigies that looked like something out of old WWII photographs taken at Belsen or Auschwitz.

And all of them were vying for the attention of those they resembled. It seemed to me that all these faint doppelgangers wanted was some kind of confirmation of their own existence, a word, a glance, a gesture…

But what where they? Ghosts? If so, why did they look like mutated versions of the people they were stalking? And what the hell did they want anyway?

It didn't take long for me to construct a plausible theory.

Night fell, and I found myself walking down by the river. The moon smeared the water with a silverish glaze, and I could hear little waves breaking on the litter-lined shore. I looked up at the underside of the High Level Bridge, the rusty steel beams, the weird tatty pieces of rope that were tied to stanchions like so many unused methods of suicide. My thoughts wandered through that barren landscape, looking for clues.

What if they were the ghosts of our selves, haunting their corporeal vessels? The sides of us that we neglect in the blind headlong rush into modernity and empty consumerism — the creative side, the caring side, the untended part of us that isn't so hard-bitten and jaded.

And what if they are *fading* as our society becomes harder, harsher, more insular? As we lose our empathy for others, our sense of being more than just another rat in the race, what if these other, softer selves are gradually being reduced to nothing; mere suggestions of shadows on the wall, hushed noises in the night?

When we see a ghost, we are actually seeing ourselves, a

forgotten part of our humanity left to rot, to grow stale and listless. That is why phantoms are always so familiar; and instead of realising the truth, we assume that we have seen the spirits of long-dead friends and relatives, when in reality we are catching a glimpse of ourselves. Each of us is haunted, but few of us ever stand still long enough to ask why, or by whom.

It takes too great a paradigm shift, far too much of a sideways step outside a lifetime of human conditioning, to allow us to see the truth.

I went back to High Bridge Street every weekend for the next month, hoping to catch sight of her getting out of another taxi outside another expensive clothes shop. Last time I hadn't been paying sufficient attention; next time I would make sure.

Finally she came back, this time with a friend — some other bored middle-class *hausfrau* looking to spend her partner's hard-earned crust on a late-night shopping trip. When she stepped out onto the rain-shined pavement, I turned quickly away, employing peripheral vision.

And there it was, sitting on her shoulders like a grim little monkey: a heavily creased, semi-transparent entity, beating her about the head and the back of the neck and trying desperately to gain her attention. Its face was small, dried-up and wrinkled like a raisin, its hands twisted into tough claws. It was a part of her that was now lost forever, a single shard of her psyche screaming into the void that was slowly swallowing it up.

And my ex wife couldn't see it at all.

I walked away into drizzle and near-darkness, catching sight of my reflection in a wet shop window. I watched myself watching myself, taking note of every detail, each tiny flaw in the sum of my parts. The picture that stared back at me seemed to intensify briefly, gaining substance for a moment. Then the traffic noise and the toneless chatter of those around me pulled me back into the land of the not-quite living. The reflection was simply that: an inverted image of a dirty man on a wet street.

The Unseen

There is hope left for some, the one's whose ghosts are reasonably intact, and who are aware enough to nurture the essence of what it is to be truly alive. But for those whose humanity is already frail, battered and etiolated, there is no hope left at all.

PUMPKIN NIGHT

*"Men fear death as children fear to go in the dark; and as that natural
fear in children is increased with tales, so is the other."*

Sir Francis Bacon, "Of Death"
Essays (1625)

The pumpkin, faceless and eyeless, yet nonetheless intimidating,
glared up at Baxter as he sat down opposite with the knife.

He had cleared a space on the kitchen table earlier in the day,
putting away the old photographs, train tickets, and receipts from
restaurants they had dined at over the years. Katy had kept these
items in a large cigar box under their bed, and he had always
mocked her for the unlikely sentimentality of the act. But now that
she was dead, he silently thanked her for having such forethought.

He fingered the creased, leathery surface of the big pumpkin,
imagining how it might look when he was done. Every Halloween
Katy had insisted upon the ritual, something begun in her family
when she was a little girl. A carved pumpkin, the task undertaken
by the man of the house; the seeds and pithy insides scooped out
into a bowl and used for soup the next day. Katy had always loved
Halloween, but not in a pathetic Goth-girl kind of way. She always
said that it was the only time of the year she felt part of something,
and rather than ghosts and goblins she felt the presence of human

wrongdoing near at hand.

He placed the knife on the table, felt empty tears welling behind his eyes.

Rain spat at the windows, thunder rumbled overhead. The weather had taken a turn for the worse only yesterday, as if gearing up for a night of spooks. Outside, someone screamed. Laughter. The sound of light footsteps running past his garden gate but not stopping, never stopping here.

The festivities had already started. If he was not careful, Baxter would miss all the fun.

The first cut was the deepest, shearing off the top of the pumpkin to reveal the substantial material at its core. He sliced around the inner perimeter, levering loose the bulk of the meat. With great care and dedication, he managed to transfer it to the glass bowl. Juices spilled onto the tablecloth, and Baxter was careful not to think about fresh blood dripping onto creased school uniforms.

Fifteen minutes later he had the hollowed-out pumpkin before him, waiting for a face. He recalled her features perfectly, his memory having never failed to retain the finer details of her scrunched-up nose, the freckles across her forehead, the way her mouth tilted to one side when she smiled. Such a pretty face, one that fooled everyone; and hiding behind it were such *unconventional* desires.

Hesitantly, he began to cut.

The eyeholes came first, allowing her to see as he carried out the rest of the work. Then there was the mouth, a long, graceful gouge at the base of the skull. She smiled. He blinked, taken by surprise. In his dreams, it had never been so easy.

Hands working like those of an Italian Master, he finished the sculpture. The rain intensified, threatening to break the glass of the large kitchen window. More children capered by in the night, their catcalls and yells of "Trick or treat!" like music to his ears.

The pumpkin did not speak. It was simply a vegetable with wounds for a face. But it smiled, and it waited, a noble and intimidating presence inhabiting it.

"I love you," said Baxter, standing and leaning towards the pumpkin. He caressed it with steady hands, his fingers finding the furrows and crinkles that felt nothing like Katy's smooth, smooth face. But it would do, this copy, this effigy. It would serve a purpose far greater than himself.

Picking up the pumpkin, he carried it to the door. Undid the locks. Opened it to let in the night. Voices carried on the busy air, promising a night of carnival, and the sky lowered to meet him as he walked outside and placed Katy's pumpkin on the porch handrail, the low flat roof protecting it from the rain.

He returned inside for the candle. When he placed it inside the carved head, his hands at last began to shake. Lighting the wick was difficult, but he persevered. He had no choice. Her hold on him, even now, was too strong to deny. For years he had covered up her crimes, until he had fallen in line with her and joined in the games she played with the lost children, the ones who nobody ever missed.

Before long, he loved it as much as she did, and his old way of life had become nothing but a rumour of normality.

The candle flame flickered, teased by the wind, but the rain could not reach it. Baxter watched in awe as it flared, licking out of the eyeholes to lightly singe the side of the face. The pumpkin smiled again, and then its mouth twisted into a parody of laughter.

Still, there were no sounds, but he was almost glad of that. To hear Katy's voice emerging from the pumpkin might be too much. Reality had warped enough for now; anything more might push him over the edge into the waiting abyss.

The pumpkin swivelled on its base to stare at him, the combination of lambent candlelight and darkness lending it an obscene expression, as if it were filled with hatred. Or lust.

Baxter turned away and went inside. He left the door unlocked and sat back down at the kitchen table, resting his head in his hands.

Shortly, he turned on the radio. The DJ was playing spooky tunes to celebrate the occasion. *Werewolves of London, Bela Lugosi's Dead, Red Right Hand. . .* songs about monsters and madmen.

Pumpkin Night

Baxter listened for awhile, then turned off the music, went to the sink, and filled the kettle. He thought about Katy as he waited for the water to boil. The way her last days had been like some ridiculous horror film, with her bedridden and coughing up blood — her thin face transforming into a monstrous image of Death.

She had not allowed him to send for a doctor, or even call for an ambulance at the last. She was far too afraid of what they might find in the cellar, under the shallow layer of dirt. Evidence of the things they had done together, the games they had played, must never be allowed into the public domain. Schoolteacher and school caretaker, lovers, comrades in darkness, prisoners of their own desires. Their deeds, she always told him, must remain secret.

He sipped his tea and thought of better days, bloody nights, the slashed and screaming faces of the children she had loved — the ones nobody else cared for, so were easy to lure here, out of the way, to the house on the street where nobody went. Not until Halloween, when all the streets of Scarbridge, and all the towns beyond, were filled with the delicious screaming of children.

There was a sound from out on the porch, a wild thrumming, as if Katy's pumpkin was vibrating, energy building inside, the blood lust rising, rising, ready to burst in a display of savagery like nothing he had ever seen before. The pumpkin was absorbing the power of this special night, drinking in the desires of small children, the thrill of proud parents, the very idea of spectres abroad in the darkness.

It was time.

He went upstairs and into the bedroom, where she lay on the bed, waiting for him to come and fetch her. He picked her up off the old, worn quilt and carried her downstairs, being careful not to damage her further as he negotiated the narrow staircase.

When he sat her down in the chair, she tipped to one side, unsupported. The polythene rustled, but it remained in place.

Baxter went and got the pumpkin, making sure that the flame did not go out. But it never would, he knew that now. The flame would burn forever, drawing into its hungry form whatever darkness stalked the night. It was like a magnet, that flame, pulling towards itself all of human evil. It might be Halloween, but there were no such things as monsters. Just people, and the things they did to each other.

He placed the pumpkin in the sink. Then, rolling up his sleeves, he set to work on her body. He had tied the polythene bag tightly around the stump of her neck, sealing off the wound. The head had gone into the ice-filled bath, along with . . . the other things, the things he could not yet bring himself to think about.

The smell hit him as soon as he removed the bag, a heavy meaty odour that was not at all unpleasant. Just different from what he was used to.

Discarding the carrier bag, he reclaimed the pumpkin from the sink, oh-so careful not to drop it on the concrete floor. He reached out and placed it on the stub of Katy's neck, pressing down so that the tiny nubbin of spine that still peeked above the sheared cartilage of her throat entered the body of the vegetable. Grabbing it firmly on either side, a hand on each cheek, he twisted and pressed, pressed and twisted, until the pumpkin sat neatly between Katy's shoulders, locked tightly in place by the jutting few inches of bone.

The flame burned yellow, blazing eyes that tracked his movements as he stood back to inspect his work.

Something shifted, the sound carrying across the silent room — an arm moving, a shoulder shrugging, a hand flexing. Then Katy tilted her new head from side to side, as if adjusting to the fit.

Baxter walked around the table and stood beside her, just as he always had, hands by his sides, eyes wide and aching. He watched as she shook off the webs of her long sleep and slowly began to stand.

Baxter stood his ground when she leaned forward to embrace him, fumbling her loose arms around his shoulders, that great carved head looming large in his vision, blotting out the rest of the room. She smelled sickly-sweet; her breath was tainted. Her long, thin fingers raked at his shoulder blades, seeking purchase, looking for the familiar gaps in his armour, the chinks and crevices she had so painstakingly crafted during the years they had spent together.

When at last she pulled away, taking a short shuffling step back towards the chair, her mouth was agape. The candle burned within, lighting up the orange-dark interior of her new head. She vomited an orangery-pulp onto his chest, staining him. The pumpkin seeds followed — hundreds of them, rotten and oversized and surging from between her knife-cut lips to spatter on the floor in a long shiver of putrescence. And finally, there was blood. So much blood.

When the stagnant cascade came to an end, he took her by the arm and led her to the door, guiding her outside and onto the wooden-decked porch, where he sat her in the ratty wicker chair she loved so much. He left her there, staring out into the silvery veil of the rain, breathing in the shadows and the things that hid within them. Was that a chuckle he heard, squeezing from her still-wet mouth?

Maybe, for a moment, but then it was drowned out by the sound of trick-or-treaters sprinting past in the drizzly lane.

He left the door ajar, so that he might keep an eye on her. Then, still shaking slightly, he opened the refrigerator door. On the middle shelf, sitting in a shallow bowl, were the other pumpkins, the smaller ones, each the size of a tennis ball. He took one in each hand, unconsciously weighing them, and headed for the hall, climbing the stairs at an even pace, his hands becoming steady once more.

In the small room at the back of the house, on a chipboard cabinet beneath the shuttered window, there sat a large plastic dish. Standing over it, eyes cast downward and unable to lift his gaze to look inside, Baxter heard the faint rustle of polythene. He straightened and listened, his eyes glazed with tears not of sorrow but of loss, of grief, and so much more than he could even begin to fathom.

Katy had died in childbirth. Now that she was back, the twins would want to join their mother, and the games they would play together promised to be spectacular.

OWED

Lana sat on the floor, in the centre of the ransacked room, holding her face and trying not to cry. It wouldn't help for Hayley to see her in tears; the girl had already gone through far too much. She stared at the place where the television used to be, the space on the sideboard the stereo had once occupied, and was filled with such an overpowering sense of loss that it felt as if the earth beneath her might crack and split, spilling forth all the demons from her personal version of hell.

"Mummy." Hayley stood in the doorway, her pale hands clutching Mr. Bear by his well-worn ear. She had on her nightdress — it was early; still well before noon — and her long blonde hair was mussed. Her eyes were wide and bright and colourless, like those of her beloved dolls. At fourteen, she was too young to cling to these toys, but Lana didn't have the heart to show her too many of life's bitter truths — the twin realities of their terrible financial situation and Hayley's disorder were more than enough for the girl to cope with.

"I'm okay, honey. Mummy's fine." Lana's jaw ached where the man had hit her — a quick backhanded blow that knocked her off her feet — but the lie hurt her far more than a superficial injury ever could.

"Did they take the TV?"

Owed

Lana nodded; the sudden motion set stars spinning across her field of vision. "Yes, honey. They took everything." The TV, the stereo, the computer; her daughter's second-hand IPod and games console: all of it.

Hayley shifted her weight from one foot to the other, her fingers playing with the seam of Mr. Bear's ear. Her thin face looked transparent, barely there, and the bones of her shoulders showed through the thin material of her pink nightdress. Often, when Lana looked at her daughter, she felt like weeping; other times — times like this — she felt like destroying the world.

"You go back into your room and get dressed. Mummy just needs to clean up." Lana stood shakily, her eyes losing track of the room, legs quivering, and moved over to the window. She stared down at the street, glad that the long black car was gone and the goons had returned to Bright's side. "Go on now."

"Yes, Mummy." Hayley shuffled next door and began to open and close drawers, choosing what she would wear. She was bad with decisions: she would be in there for some time, staring at her clothes and agonising over each potential outfit with the door locked and bolted to keep her developing curves out of sight.

"Bastards," said Lana, under her breath. The two men had said they would be back if she didn't repay the debt in full, including the obscene amount of interest it had accrued. They'd also said that, if she no longer possessed enough goods to substitute for cash, other arrangements could be made. The salacious look in the eyes of the one who'd hit her was unmistakable; the way his partner had turned towards Hayley's room was even more disturbing.

"Bastards," she said again, but with less feeling this time. Her anger was subsiding. There was little she could do. The sky outside was growing dark and overcast; clouds were merging into a single solid mass. Rain spattered the window, gentle as baby spit, and Lana was forced to look away from the dour scene.

Two years ago she'd been working for a successful finance company in Leeds, her salary enough to afford the good things in life. Now, after a run-in with a sex pest boss, and a case of unfair dismissal she'd failed to win, she felt trapped in a life that didn't feel like her own. The small detached property Hayley was born in had been sold to pay legal fees and expenses, and the council had re-housed them here, in a tiny two-bed flat on this dismal estate situated south of the city.

Lana felt so useless. She could not even support her child, the product of a loveless encounter with an ex colleague after a work function. An alcohol-baby, sired during a moment of vodka-induced madness. And where was the father now? She didn't know, didn't care; as far as she was concerned, he might as well be dead.

The rain fell harder against the glass, sounding like tiny fingertips desperate for her attention. She slumped into an armchair — one of the few items left behind by the debt collectors — and stared at the electric fire she could no longer afford to run.

She'd borrowed a few grand from Monty Bright when there had been no other way out. Her benefits had been delayed, Hayley needed to eat, and the bills were mounting up like a paper hill in the hallway. Going to the loan shark had seemed like a practical plan: a temporary solution. Unfortunately, things had become so bad that she had needed him again. Before long, her debts were uncontrollable, growing like a living thing; metastasising like a cancer.

"Mummy. I'm ready." Hayley was standing beside her. She'd barely been aware of her daughter coming into the room.

"Ready for what, honey?" She smiled through the tears. That was all she ever did: grit her teeth and smile, pretend that everything was going to work out when she knew it wasn't.

"Anything." Hayley's eyes were wider than before. She looked dazed, as if it were she who had suffered the blow to the jaw.

"Are you okay, Hayley? You look poorly." Lana reached out, put her arms around her child, hugged her, feeling the scant warmth of her underfed body.

"The Slittens came again."

Lana stiffened. She didn't mean to, but it was a natural reaction. The doctor had told her just to go along with whatever

Hayley said, to gently change the subject, but it was easier said than done — easier discussed in an NHS office than carried out in a grubby council flat with rain on the windows and broken toys on the floor.

"Hush now, honey. You know I don't like that kind of talk." She squeezed tighter, hoping that Hayley might get the message.

"But they can help. They told me. The Slittens saw what those men did, and they say they can put things right. All you have to do is ask."

Through gritted teeth, Lana let out an uneasy laugh. "That's what they all say, honey." She buried her face in Hayley's chest, smelled her rich scent, the odour she'd been born with and that had never left her — a misplaced baby-smell that should by now have been replaced by a melange of oestrogen and cheap perfume. "We'll be fine. Everything will work out right. I promise."

Hayley tensed against her, as if she were trying to outmanoeuvre her mother's touch, to pull away without actually moving.

Lana felt like she'd just told her daughter the biggest lie of all.

Later, after tidying the room and rearranging the remaining furniture, Lana left Hayley to play with her jigsaws and headed for Monty Bright's place. She had spent the rest of the morning trying to think of another way, to formulate an alternative plan. Not long after noon, she had finally faced the truth and begun to prepare herself for a confrontation.

It was still raining when she stepped out of the building and into the street. The wooden windows of the shops opposite were dark and streaky, reflecting dense banks of cloud; the glass panes had still not been replaced from when local kids had thrown empty beer bottles through them a fortnight ago. Young people in tracksuits and hooded sweatshirts gathered on corners and in doorways, their faces featureless smudges against a flat grey background.

She followed the narrow lanes that led to the row of shops

where Bright kept his offices. The environment deteriorated around her: buildings low and stooped, windows broken or boarded. Soon she was standing at the kerb outside a shut-up bookmaker's. A light shone sickly and weak from an upstairs window. The sign over the recessed door had been sprayed with whorls of black paint, its text long since obliterated. Even the graffiti in these parts was meaningless.

Lana reached out a shaking hand and pressed the buzzer. It was set into a metal plate that had seen better times. A low droning sounded somewhere deep inside the building, like the mournful call of an ailing elephant. Lana closed her eyes, pressed her fingernails into the meat of her palms.

"*It'll be okay,*" she whispered. "*Be fine.*"

The door banged open, slamming against its frame. "What you want?"

Lana opened her eyes and stared at the man on the doorstep. He was huge — well over six feet tall — and his head was shaved right down to the glistening flesh of his scalp. His eyes were narrow, untrusting, and a black snake tattoo ran around his skull, an inch above his ears.

"Well, bitch?"

Lana took a step back, feeling a breeze press against her legs. She wanted to run but knew that she could not. "I'm here to see Monty Bright. My name is Lana Temple."

The big man laughed; his shoulders rolled in a strange loose movement. "Lot of people want to see Monty. He's a popular guy, especially with the bitches." His smile was all gold teeth.

"Just tell him my name, fuckwit. He'll want to see me, I'm sure."

The man leaned backwards, momentarily shocked, and then smiled again. "Stay there." The door slammed shut.

Minutes later she was climbing a dingy stairwell. Three floors: a landing on each, with doors that led into tawdry boudoirs and chambers of ill-repute. Behind the closed doors she heard abrasive laughter; the open ones showed her skinny women clad in male-fantasy underwear; sluttish scraps of red-and-black lace. Bruised smiles and empty stares.

"This way," said the big man, stepping aside when at last they reached the top floor. The muscles bulged beneath his thin white T-shirt and his tight jeans showed a similar bulge at the crotch that was nothing short of terrifying. He cupped his balls and grinned, flashing once again those ugly gold teeth. "Go on in."

Lana pushed open the door and stepped into a room that was bare, functional, but surprisingly tasteful. Framed shop-bought Monet prints hung on the walls, the pile of the carpet was thick and plush, and the furniture was all real leather. Monty Bright sat behind a long oak desk, leafing through a pornographic magazine. The cover showed a woman, bound and gagged, being penetrated by a large black man with a thick penis. Bright's orange oval face shone with thinly disguised delight. His slick black hair looked like a shell or a carapace.

She stood in the centre of the room and waited to be noticed. Her hands toyed with the hem of her jacket. A wall-mounted clock loudly ticked away the seconds.

"Hello Lana," he said without glancing up, away from the images of bondage and humiliation. His long thin hands turned the pages, his dark eyes consuming rather than seeing what they flicked across with an animal intensity. "How can I help?"

He'd said the same thing when she'd first approached him for money: it was his catchphrase; an ironic combination of words that she could see amused him on some level that she could not even begin to fathom.

"I've come here... to ask for mercy."

Bright looked up from the magazine, setting it aside on the disturbingly neat and tidy desk top. Thoughtfully, he steepled his fingers under his rounded chin and examined her, as if seeing her for the first time. His teeth were short and pointed; his tanned face was unmoving, like a photograph, but as soon as he smiled the illusion wavered. "I see. Is this regarding the little visit my boys paid you this morning? I see they went against my orders and roughed you up."

"That doesn't matter. All I care about is my daughter. I'll do whatever you want, just cancel the debt and let her have a real life." The request came before she'd even begun to formulate it; deep down, this was the cold truth of her heart.

"Anything, Lana? *Anything* I want?" He opened a drawer and took out a bottle of whisky and a small shot glass. His hands were beautiful.

She glanced at the magazine, with its lurid cover. Black leather. Pink flesh. Red wounds. "Anything," she agreed, knowing that she had already sealed her fate, but hoping that her daughter's might be better.

First he watched her strip naked and bound her to a chair. He did not even take her to a private room, just called a handful of his men into the office and told them to watch. The straps he used where thin and tight; they cut deep into the skin of her arms and legs. Blood ran freely down her shins, along her forearms. She tried not to scream but could not stop herself from moaning. The pain at this point was mild but she knew it could only get worse.

"This one's a looker, Monty. A real babe." She did not see who spoke; the leather mask prevented peripheral vision.

She closed her eyes and thought about Hayley, knowing that she was securing her daughter's future. The pain she suffered here would guarantee that Hayley's life would be pain-free, at least in the *extreme* sense of the word. Any agony Hayley experienced would constitute the normal, everyday hurts, the small wounds of the masses.

She didn't even call out when he started with the whip. Nor did she weep when they took turns to rape her, using her like a slab of meat as they entered her body in so many ways and via so many different routes that soon she became numb to the tireless invasion.

"Are we done?" She buttoned her blouse, retaining a small sense of dignity even after what had been done to her. Her hair was wet and smelled of semen; they had not allowed her to bathe afterwards, just laughed at her pathetic request, as if in confirmation that she would never be clean again.

"For now." Bright sat in his chair smoking a cigar. His narrow hands were dwarfed by the fat Cuban, looked comical even. His bare feet were resting on the desk as he reclined in the seat, content in her debasement.

"What do you mean?" She stood and faced him, terror creeping upward, moving in waves across her defiled body. "You promised." But any promises this man made were subject to the whims of his radical personality. She'd been a fool to let herself believe this would make any difference to her situation; but what else did she have to cling to other than foolish belief?

"I promised nothing. Consider this visit a down payment. The way I figure it, you'll have cleared the debt in, say, fifteen to eighteen months. Even quicker if you bring the girl along next time. What's her name, Hayley? Nice and tight and pretty. I've seen her through the school gates, playing with her friends. I think *my* friends would like to play with her very much."

Lana knew that she should rush him, go for the throat, the eyes: attack the soft parts. But it was futile; he was too strong, and had always possessed the upper hand. Right from the start, he'd played her along, upping the odds until she came to him and offered him exactly what he wanted and could have taken at any point. But he did not want to take; it was the very act of *offering* that turned him on, made him shine.

"Where's your compassion?" she said, failing to penetrate his armour. "Your basic human decency?" She hated the desperation in her voice, but it was all she had left to offer.

Bright stood and came out from behind the desk. He was shorter than she remembered in his stocking feet; barely came up to her shoulder once she'd put on her heels. His skin looked soft, malleable, and his eyes protruded like boiled eggs from a face as flat and round as a polished plate. Bright's shoulders were hunched; his posture was awkward, as if years of ingesting horse steroids and the mindless repetition of punishing routines with heavy weights had altered his basic body shape. He slowly raised his hands and began to slip off his shirt.

"For that, dear Lana, I'd have to be human."

The leather mask had prevented her from seeing it before, but his naked body was a mass of lumps and abrasions. They looked like ripe tumours: they dangled in clumps from beneath his armpits, clustered around his nipples; made a ribbed embossment down his hairless belly. There were mouths in there, amid the globules and curlicues of flesh, and eyes that blinked uncomprehendingly. A nose or a sex gland twitched; snot or semen spilled from its shiny, puckered end. It was a whole community of beings, perhaps even the souls of the people he'd absorbed as repayment for debts even greater than her own, loans whose rate of interest was infinite.

"Bring the girl next time. I'll show her a whole new world of hurt."

She was surprised he didn't try to stop her as she fled. The door was unlocked and there was no one on the landing. She clattered down the wooden stairs in her too-high heels and almost fell out of the main door when it opened at her touch. She could hear Bright's laughter following her as she ran along the dark street, looking for answers to questions she could not even remember asking.

Hayley was in the living room when she got back to the flat, sitting with her legs crossed and watching the empty space where they TV had always stood. Lana went to her daughter, but the girl seemed dazed, out of it. Lana checked her arms for track marks, opened her mouth and looked inside for the powder traces of pills. She found nothing, so assumed this fugue was simply another symptom of her disorder, the condition the doctors consistently failed to explain.

Finally, she carried Hayley through to her room and lay her down on the single bed, pulling the covers over her frail form and kissing her sweat-slick forehead. Sirens wailed in the distance, tracking criminals along shadowy streets. Someone screamed a name, over and over again, but Lana could not make out what it was. Eventually the shouting faded, but the backbeat of dance music drifted on the evening air, its sonorous moan synching with the rhythm of the blood as it throbbed in her veins.

Lana left her daughter and went to the bathroom. She ran a bath and stood naked by the tub while it filled, staring at her reflection in the steaming mirror. She lay in the bath and let the badness boil out of her; the water buoyed her, kept her in the world, floating like a dead fish. After scrubbing her flesh, inside and out, she sat up and took the razor blade from the shelf, where it lay behind an old bottle of baby lotion.

She stared at the veins on her wrists, wondering if she would ever be able to do it. Then, carefully, she began the ritual. She gently pressed the blade against the papery skin, turning it through ninety degrees to make the sign of a cross at the point where palm became wrist. White marks, fading like the memories of the life she'd had before. No blood, just a slight pressure, a reminder that a solution was always there, waiting beneath the surface.

She put away the blade and submerged herself, listening to the odd sound of water in her ears.

After her bath, she dressed in clean clothes and returned to Hayley's room. The girl was still sleeping, lying in exactly the same position as when Lana had left her. The girl's eyes moved rapidly beneath waxy lids; she was seeing something different than the depressing sights around her. Maybe even something wonderful.

Lana leaned over and watched her daughter's sleeping face.

"I'm sorry, honey. Mummy couldn't make it better." Tears ran down her cheeks and she stroked Hayley's cold cheek. "I tried, I really did, but I couldn't manage it. I'm sorry for your illness, I'm sorry for the things we've seen and done. I'm sorry your daddy isn't around to see how beautiful you are."

Hayley's eyelids flickered, and then slowly opened. Her eyes were completely white, without a trace of pupil or iris. She opened her mouth and a trail of saliva ran down her chin.

"Oh, Hayley. Oh, honey." Lana cradled her child in her arms and reached out to something she didn't believe in. If there was a

God, or some kind of greater power that watched over the fallen, then why would it not answer her pleas?

"The Slitten," said Hayley, her voice low and cold and even. "They will help. Just ask. *Ask.*"

After everything she'd seen today, Lana was ready to believe in anything; any slim hope offered to her looked appealing, even the private fantasy of a damaged teenager. She let go of Hayley and fell to her knees at the side of the bed, clasping her hands in prayer. She lowered her head and gathered whatever energy still inhabited her battered body.

"*Just ask.*" Hayley's voice was a whisper, an echo.

"Help me. Please help." Lana's voice sounded different, felt strange as it left her throat. The words were like solid objects regurgitated into the room. They had shape and form and dimensional properties: they were alive, and went out in search of something incredible.

Hayley was sitting up in bed when Lana opened her eyes. The expression on her daughter's face was one of bliss, like a child on Christmas morning. She held her hands together in front of her chest, and then slowly, and with great intent, she unbuttoned her nightdress.

Lana leaned back, and then moved forward. "What are you doing, honey?" The hope was gone; the belief was spent. There was nothing here but a girl who had lost touch with reality and a mother who had failed to protect her.

"I'm *summoning* them." Hayley's breasts were bigger than she expected; they spilled out of the open neck of the garment, full and firm and lactating. Watery milk striated with pale crimson streaks leaked from the rigid nipples, drawing wet lines down Hayley's bloodless, paper-thin chest.

Rain hammered at the windows, but it wasn't raining; hadn't rained for hours. Shadows streaked the walls and ceiling; the bricks and floorboards creaked as if in preparation for the arrival of something glorious. The air turned dusty, grey light seeping from invisible cracks to baptise the room.

Light webbing drifted down from the ceiling, like the web of a spider, but longer, firmer, thicker. At the top of each frosted strand there was a small bundle which began to unfurl. Dusty petals opening. Striving for the light.

"What are they?"

"The Slitten." Hayley bared her chest to the room, throwing back her head and closing her eyes in an expression of near ecstasy. The Slitten responded *en masse*; scores of them dropped like desiccated spiders from the ceiling, rolling across the floor towards the bed. They were shadow and half-light, lines and slashes, more thought than substance. Their features were vague, like stolen shards of daylight trapped in sealed rooms, and their limbs were many and sharp-clawed.

Lana suddenly realised why Hayley never wanted to undress in front of her — it was not, as she had thought, a simple case of teenage modesty, but an attempt to hide her saggy little belly, engorged breasts and long, red-leaking nipples... to conceal the fact of her recent motherhood. The baggy clothes, the moodiness, the increasing secrecy — it all made sense now, at last, in terms of this virgin birth.

The Slitten crawled up onto the bed, swarming over her daughter and obscuring her lower torso. They reached up and began to suckle, taking it in turns to slake a thirst born in darkness. Lana watched in awe; her daughter was a mother to monsters, and for some reason the thought did not fill her with terror. Instead, she felt a sense of purpose.

Soon the Slitten were satisfied; they rolled off Hayley and gathered around Lana, their movements slow and heavy.

"Ask them," said a voice from the bed, in the shadows. "Ask them again."

Lana reached out her hands, and began to speak.

Some time in the early hours, not long before the blood-red wash of dawn, Lana once again left the relative safety of the flat. Hayley was sleeping, worn out by the night's demands on her young body. Lana's wounds ached, but she was tough enough to ignore the pain.

Beneath Lana's long winter coat, the Slitten — her grandchildren — had attached themselves to her body, pumping resolve into her system while supping the life from her veins. She was a being of contrasts: guardian and wet nurse, victim and criminal; strength and fragility, darkness and light.

Crossing the road, she allowed herself the brief indulgence of imagining Bright's face when he saw her, his look of horror when she opened her coat to show him what he and his perversions had helped sire.

This time she would not succumb to his distasteful demands.

This time, as requested, a debt would be paid in full.

WHY GHOSTS WAIL:
A BRIEF MEMOIR

It was a dry, overcast Tuesday evening in the cold mid winter when I came back from the dead. Night was falling in slow shades from a sky that looked flat and grey as old slate.

I hauled myself from the river in which I'd drowned over a year ago — losing control of my car on an invisible sheet of black ice and plummeting to a watery demise — and stood on the muddy bank. Dripping.

The moon was heavy and bloated, drooping through the thin clouds like a pregnant woman's belly and birthing a cold, hard light that did little to illuminate the way. I stared at the surrounding countryside, noting how much it had changed in my absence. Trees were bent and crippled, sporting layers of powdery mould from some ferocious blight; grass was brown and spiky, starved of moisture and sunlight; even the water from which I'd risen ran thick and black as crude oil.

Everything seemed tainted, polluted.

I walked in the direction of my old house, planning to look in on Molly and the kids. I didn't plan to haunt them; that would only cause them alarm. No, I just wanted to check that they were surviving their grief, and that their lives were back on track since my small, ill-attended funeral. I wanted to see that they were okay.

I passed O'Malley's place and saw old Tom crawling around in the mud outside the empty ruins of his family farm. He was down on all fours, like one of the animals he'd bred back when he was still among the living, and stuffing great handfuls of mud into his mouth. Tom's face was drawn and elongated, his mouth stretched open like a grain sack. It made him look like that old painting, *The Scream*.

The clumped dirt just poured through him, returning to the ground where it had originated, leaving no trace on his transparent form. Tom had been dead for five years.

Tom's wife and son had left the area not long after they'd buried him, relocating to New Zealand. Their absence must have driven Tom's wraith insane, and all he could do to be near them was ram fistfuls of the earth they'd loved into his maw.

The dead have boundaries, lines and borders that cannot be crossed. We are tied to *places*, not people; and sometimes those we leave behind move on to destinations where we are unable to follow.

I averted my eyes and moved on. I had no desire to attract Tom's attention, or to disturb what must be his nightly ordeal. Unstable spectral images of livestock that had been culled during the last B.S.E scare flickered in and out of focus around him, like a weird strobe effect. Tom reached out for them with mud-spattered hands, but the cows vanished before he could make any kind of contact, only to reappear elsewhere in the field, as if teasing him, or playing some kind of ghostly game of tag.

My clothes refused to dry as I walked, and my skin remained grey-white and sodden, the colour and texture of damp tripe. A consequence of my return, I thought. I didn't even pause to wonder why I'd been allowed back into the land of the living, just accepted that I was there. To paraphrase a classic, there are far stranger things in heaven and earth than my limited philosophy can comprehend.

I passed not a single car as I trod the narrow and winding road to the cottage; nor did I see any other pedestrians braving the chill night air. Whether anyone would have been able to see me is a question that I cannot answer. Perhaps, I thought then, only those dear to me might perceive my presence. Or perhaps were I to enter a building, I'd register only as a faint wind in the room despite closed doors and windows, a sudden chill in the air, a partially glimpsed movement in an otherwise empty chamber.

The little rose garden I'd tended in life was overgrown and stricken with weeds, the plants and flowers all gone brown and rotten. Things had been left to die, just like I'd done. I guessed that Molly must still be deep in mourning to allow things to slide in this way.

The lights were on in the cottage, and I could see dim figures bobbing behind the dirty windows. The front door was chipped, the paint peeling like scabs from damaged flesh; even the bricks were flaking away, shedding in great patches like dry, reddened epidermis.

This was the house we'd bought together three months after the wedding, the place where Molly had given birth to our children, and where we'd begun to raise them. And here it was falling apart at the seams, sinking deeper and deeper into a mess of disrepair and neglect.

The state of the house seemed to reflect the condition of my wasted mortal remains when they were put in the ground, and of the three broken hearts that it held within its crumbling walls.

I glided right through the battered wooden door, passing into the house on a current of stale air that rushed to aid my transition from one place to the next.

My young son, Gary, was in the process of climbing the stairs, a moth-eaten old teddy bear in one hand, and a glass of water gripped tightly in the other. As if sensing his daddy's spirit, the boy stopped, turned. Gazed down into the dark hallway.

I screamed but no sound came. Only dark water leaking from the sides of my mouth.

Gary's face was prematurely aged, his eyes sunken into a haggard midget's skull. His pretty blonde hair was thin and wispy, falling out in dry clumps. He'd become an old, old man looking out from the body of a four-year-old boy.

I went through into the lounge when my son resumed his steady ascent to the first floor, and saw my three-year-old daughter sitting before a flickering television screen. There was a framed photograph of me on the low table beside her — a portrait taken long ago, when she was just a babe-in-arms.

One of Katie's arms was dangling slack at the shoulder, the joint having jumped, or been pulled, from its socket. The right-hand side of her face was crumpled inwards, as if from a heavy impact, and her remaining eye was staring blankly, milky-white as marble, from all that ruin.

I tried to cry, but only more stagnant river water poured from my useless tear ducts: it seems that the dead don't cry for the living. I felt only an echo of a greater despair; an ironically *phantom* feeling that haunted the inner sanctum of my being.

Molly entered the room, looking groomed and beautiful in a pair of dark blue jeans and a white woollen sweater. She was the only point of brightness in a dim landscape, the only thing that looked as I remembered. My wife. My lovely living wife.

"Molly," I tried to say, but only succeeded in sending a violent draught of air across the room, slamming the door behind her. She couldn't hear me, or sense me; even the closing of the door had gone unnoticed. In that brief moment I felt far less than even the ghost that I am.

Then Molly turned partially away from me, and bent down to offer Katie a cookie from the open pack that she held in her delicate veiny hands. Her distant gaze fluttered like an insubstantial airborne insect and came to rest upon my picture. I could see the pulse beating rapidly in her neck, as if an invisible finger was repeatedly pressing her there. As she turned back towards me her eyes were moist, and she quickly wiped them dry on the sleeve of her sweater.

A large fist-sized tumour was suspended on rubbery strings of matter, dangling from a gaping rent in Molly's back, located in the area near the kidney. The roughly circular cluster of angry cells twitched; evil, malignant, expanding in diameter as I stood there and watched.

I raised my hands to my river-wet face, and they passed straight through my head to meet empty air on the other side. Nothing could erase the awful sight.

Is it any wonder that ghosts are always seen moaning and wailing and mournful, their faces twisted and fixed into expressions of perpetual terror? When glimpsed by the living, spectres are never smiling, waving blithely, or radiating an aura of happiness.

And I'll tell you why.

Because this is what they see: the whole wide world winding down like a big old clock, everything turning to ruin, and their loved ones gradually assuming the aspect of how they will eventually pass away... little Gary from merciful old age, Katie beaten to death in her early twenties by some late-night assailant or would-be rapist, Molly quite soon from a cancer that hangs like a monkey on her back and will never, ever stop until it has devoured her.

And *I* could see it all too: what little future they had mapped out across the pale white parchment of their living, breathing bodies. I could see far too much, and they didn't even know I was there. But I had faith that they would see me eventually, catching sight of my tired spectral form whenever the pain and the rage allowed me to momentarily pass through the veil that divides us.

I tucked my legs up under my body, and slowly lowered myself down onto the floor, being very careful not to pass through the dusty carpet and creaky timber joists into the dank basement below.

And now I sit and watch the slow dissolution of those that I cherish, waiting for them to cross over. Wishing that time and space would just grind to a halt and freeze them there, in living poses, so that they no longer have to die. The other side, you see, is worse than where they are. Far, far worse than where *you* are.

One of these days I know my wife will join me, slipping her tiny ice-cold hand into mine as I stand watching our children weep. And we'll wait together, Molly and me, wailing into the emptiness, trying our hardest to warn the rest of the family; and attempting to tell them to get on and live their lives before it's too damn late to make any difference, any difference at all.

ACCIDENTAL DAMAGE

After the road accident, things began to change for Chester. It was not just a question of his perceptions — how he viewed the world — it was other things, tangible things. Like the way Lucy had stopped coming around, and his friends no longer telephoned to see how he was. Always a solitary man, Chester did not crave the attention of sick-bed revellers; he simply wanted his friends and lover to show some concern.

Maybe it was the scars. The doctors had shaved his head for the surgery, which made him look dim and thuggish, and the shiny white scar tissue traced a thick band across the top of his scalp, down over his forehead, to terminate at a point between his eyes at the bridge of his nose. It was an ugly injury, and he'd been told that the damage would never fully fade. He was scarred for life, tattooed with a physical memory of the accident in which he'd almost perished.

His actual memories of what had happened were vague, nebulous. All he could recall was driving back from Lucy's place at the other end of town two weeks before Christmas. It was late; they'd argued over something he could not remember and which she had not mentioned since he'd regained consciousness. It was dark, cold. The roads were icy. The police thought he must have hit a patch of black ice; the back roads were known to be treacherous with it every winter. All Chester knew was that he'd suddenly lost control of the car, and had then been swallowed by blackness.

He climbed out of bed, pushing aside the books and magazines that littered the area around him, and went to the window. The day was grey; the sky shimmered like sheet metal. The fields around the house seemed to close in, narrowing his world to the immediate area outside his door, but he was all too aware that this effect was merely a reflection of his psychological state.

The winter-stunted trees shook like skinny figures, their branches twitching in a slight breeze, and he glimpsed a dark shape gliding across the flattened horizon. Was it very small, like a gnat stuck on the glass, or simply far away? He could not be sure: nothing seemed stable since the accident, even his sense of self. The shape grew in size, as if either bloating or drawing near, and then it vanished, perhaps an animal ducking into a burrow or nest at the edge of a field.

It took a few minutes for Chester to realise the ringing in his head was the sound of the telephone downstairs, its shrill voice nagging to be answered.

"Who's this?" he said, hoping it was Lucy, perhaps calling to ask if she could come to the house. He left the room, catching sight of himself in the wall-mounted mirror on the landing — long, thin face, scratchy patches of partially re-grown hair on his head, wide stripes of scar tissue — and inched down the stairs, all too aware that any sudden movement might bring on one of his headaches. The stairs creaked, the banister shifted beneath his hand, his legs wobbled as he attempted to reach the phone before it rang off.

Slamming into the doorframe, he entered the lounge, and just as he lunged for the phone it stopped ringing. The silence it left behind vibrated like a tuning fork; Chester's ears stung. He picked up the receiver. "Hello. Lucy?"

Nothing but static greeted him. It sounded like the shifting of ice floes, the cracking of glaciers. Chester gripped the cold plastic, his hands weak and unable to apply much pressure. The static cleared and he heard a series of distant clicking sounds, like the swift closing of a bird's beak or the snapping of teeth. Then the line went dead.

Later that day, after a light lunch, he watched some television. The local news station was broadcasting a piece about a nearby farm where human remains had been discovered, half-frozen and buried in shallow graves. The farmer had been arrested before Christmas, when the bodies were first uncovered, but the news station replayed old footage of open graves and gave empty updates every day. They seemed obsessed with the events at the farmhouse, despite there being very little fresh news to impart. The farmer was awaiting trial but was reported to be so frail that he might not last that long. A relatively young man of forty-seven, he was said to look closer to eighty years old.

Chester watched as a tall, grey-haired anchorman walked from room to room in the old farmhouse, pointing out the strange graffiti daubed on the walls, annotated entomological sketches of insects torn from text books and hung with pins, piles of books and dirty clothing stacked against the doors and windows. The kitchen sink was thick with filth; the plates stacked there teemed with cockroaches. Strange stone carvings sat on every available surface: on shelves, benches, even on the floor, standing against the skirting boards.

"Mr. Winchester lived alone, and still denies all knowledge of the remains. The victims were killed a long time ago, and if he is indeed guilty of the murders of these people, he either stopped killing or found somewhere else to store the bodies long before his secret was uncovered."

Chester turned off the television and stared at the wall above the screen. It was as if good news was no longer worth reporting. All he ever saw or heard or read about was murder, violence and bloodshed.

He took some pain killers for his head and stood at the back door smoking a menthol cigarette. He remembered giving up smoking this time last year, but after his surgery had started up again, seeking solace in the smoke that even now filled his lungs with thin, coiling fingers. The sun was a washed-out smear in the sky, and clouds shunted each other like dodgem cars at a funfair. A single bird flew in ever-decreasing circles above the roof of the house, and he watched it as the cigarette burned down to ash in his hand.

He turned around and went inside, making a decision. If Lucy would not come to him, he would go to her. He put on his heavy coat and left the house, climbing into the four-wheel drive. It wasn't the first time he'd driven since the accident, but he had deliberately kept away from the vehicle, and whenever he was forced behind the wheel he kept to the side roads, his speed considerably lower than the legal limit.

Chester started the engine and sat at the kerb, wondering where it had all gone wrong. Before the accident, his life had been on course. The house was an inheritance from his elder sister, a spinster — left to him, along with substantial funds, when she finally lost her battle with cancer three years ago. His job was going well; Lucy was all over him, almost clamouring for his touch. Then, in a cosmic finger-snap, everything had changed. Darkness had flooded in.

He covered the miles slowly, concentrating so hard on the road ahead that a sharp pain flared up behind his eyes. The town was silent as he passed through, everyone indoors and still enjoying the remnants of the festive period. Decorations that had not yet been taken down hung limply from lampposts and road signs. The ache in his head receded to a dull throb, matching the rhythm of the traffic lights as they phased through their sequence.

When he reached Lucy's place he remained inside the car, engine running, fingers clasping the steering wheel. The radio was playing quietly, a gentle country ballad. Chester closed his eyes and willed away the pain. His arms and shoulders ached from gripping the wheel so tightly during his journey, and he felt like he was learning things all over again.

Finally he got out of the car and shuffled down Lucy's drive. The snow was melting, turning to grey slush, and withered bedding plants poked their heads through the softening crust.

He knocked on the door and waited, wishing now that he'd

called to prepare her for his visit. Lucy didn't like surprises; she was an ordered girl, with well defined edges to her world.

Her face was pale when it peeked chastely around the edge of the door, her eyes big and dark and even a little afraid. "Chester?" The sound of buzzing flies emanated from the house behind her, as if they were clustering about spoiled meat; or perhaps Lucy had simply left a noisy kitchen appliance running in the kitchen.

He watched her breath mist white in the chilled air, shrouding her features. "Hi, Lucy. I'm sorry I didn't ring, but I needed to see you." His feet crunched on leftover snow as he adjusted his position on the doorstep.

"But I thought we sorted all this out during our last conversation, Chester. That I wasn't going to come over again."

The buzzing sound grew momentarily louder, then stopped.

Chester did not know what to say. He could recall no such conversation, but to admit the fact might lead him down a road he did not want to travel. "That's why I came to you."

Lucy blinked; her eyes were all pupil, and they sucked in the light. She opened the door further until it pulled on the security chain. Chester could not remember there being a security chain in place on any of the many times he'd been here before. Had she had it fitted because of him? Absently, he rubbed at the scar tissue above his eyes with his fingertips. The raw flesh ached; it felt warm to the touch, despite the rest of his face being cold.

"What do you want, Chester?" her voice was shaky as she backed away from the door, easing it closed. "Please. Just go away. If you have any more of those relics with you, I don't want them. What the hell kind of Christmas present was that meant to be, anyway?" Her facial expression looked on the verge of hysteria, but Chester could not be sure whether she was about to laugh or scream.

He had no idea what she meant, and the pain in his head threatened to return in force. "Lucy..." But he could say nothing more; words failed him; he was bereft of ideas.

Lucy closed the door. He heard the bolts as she slid them home; and the buzzing sound recommenced, louder this time, almost avid in its intensity.

Chester stood on the doorstep for a moment or two more, lost in his own confusion, and then he turned and stalked back towards the car. A movement caught his eye, and as he glanced over at the houses opposite, he saw something lithe and dark struggling beneath a neighbour's porch, its thin hind legs scrabbling in the grubby snow. It might have been a large house pet, but for the fact that it looked spiny and elongated, and as a result of its frantic motion the thing seemed to possess more limbs than were necessary.

Chester sat behind the wheel and shook his head. His scars were livid in the rear-view mirror. He started the engine and crawled back the way he'd come, pointing the car in the right direction and hoping that he did not hit anything. On his side of town, past the old Shell garage and the small construction site that never seemed to progress beyond the demolition stage, he passed the tree he'd hit in the accident. He slowed down without realising, stopped and got out of the car.

The tree had a huge split in its trunk, near the thick roots where they poked through the earth like fat fingers. The cleft was dark, moist, and looked as if it might be deep enough to lead into the centre of the earth. Chester got down on his knees and stared into the hole, aware that from a distance it might appear that he was praying. He smiled, placed the fingers of one hand inside the hole, brushing its sides. Someone had stuffed snow in there, perhaps a passing child. His fingers burrowed into the soft layer, and he grasped something. When he pulled out the object he saw that it was a child's doll, a mere plaything. The doll was naked; the smooth plastic of its body was gouged and bitten, possibly during rough play, and its hair had been clumsily removed. Its glass eyeballs remained intact, but they had been damaged with a thin blade or the pointed ends of sharp, needle-like teeth.

"Jesus," he said, throwing the doll as far away from himself as he could. It landed on the soft snow, face-down, as if trying to burrow back into the earth. Beyond it, in the distance, three or four sleek shapes dropped down from an upright position and began to caper in a brown field patched with white. They ran in circles, chasing or being chased, and as Chester squinted into the low winter sun, the shapes seemed to diminish, bleeding into the background like ink stains.

Chester forced his hand once more into the cleft in the tree, and when he withdrew it he was holding two small items wrapped in crumpled piece of paper. When he opened the package he realised the wrapping was in fact a child's crayon drawing of a house. It contained a pair of figures carved crudely from stone.

Relics.

Were these the same as the ones Lucy had accused him of offering her, and if so, what were their purpose? They were tiny, their outlines uncertain, and each one had too many arms and legs to be considered wholly human. Although the figures were standing upright, they looked as if they'd be more comfortable scrabbling around closer to the ground.

That evening he was unable to eat dinner. His appetite had been quashed by the situation with Lucy. He tried to remember what had occurred between them, but all he could summon was the image of her back, retreating along the footpath towards her car. Had they argued again? Had he struck out at her? Now that he thought about it, when she'd peeked at him around the edge of the door earlier that day, it had looked like she was sporting a black eye.

His sister's house settled around him, groaning and popping like an old man's joints. Something that sounded like tiny footsteps scurried across the underside of the floorboards in the hall. Chester gazed out of the lounge window, watching the sun go down across the fields, the light fleeing from him, as if sucked back into that great dying star. The darkness left in its place shivered with potential movement and he closed the curtains to block out the view.

He stood by the mirror and examined his features. He no longer looked like himself; his face was twisted out of shape. The scars shone, catching the last of the dying light, and when the ceiling lamp flickered, the taut strips of tissue seemed to jump from his head and hover in the air like ectoplasm. Even when he closed his eyes he could see his altered image: mouth pulled into a grimace, eyes set too far apart, cheeks fuzzed with beard growth to compensate for the lack of hair on his head.

He often thought that, during the accident, when his head had cracked open on the windscreen, something had crawled out: some inner darkness he had freed inadvertently into the external world. Then, on bad days, he thought that maybe it was the other way around and something had crawled inside, taking up residence in his broken skull.

His brain twitched, but he pushed the image away. There was nothing in there but a complex bundle of nerve endings and highly responsive matter; even his thoughts had abandoned him.

Leaning into the mirror, he stared at his eyes, and was shocked to see movement behind them. Like looking through a window, he glimpsed a large dark mass as it passed across his gaze, turning to notice him for a second.

"*No*," he whispered. "*No*."

Running to the front door, he opened it and glared out into the evening, watching the distant shapes as they cavorted like children in the growing gloom. They snapped at each other, massive mandibles compressing only empty air, newly muscled bodies twisting in the twilight as they drew closer to the house, where they had been headed all along. Had he unleashed these things during the accident, or had they simply been lying in wait, preparing for the right moment to escape the cage of his mind?

He slammed the door, pushed a chair against it, then stood back and wondered how strong they were. He gathered other items of furniture from the lounge and heaved them against the door to prevent them from entering — an antique bureau, a set of drawers, the moth-eaten settee. Then, panting, he sat on the bottom stair and watched the door, sensing their approach, calculating how long it might take them to break down his flimsy barricade.

His balance failed him as he tried to stand, and he reached out to steady himself on the banister. Upstairs, something moved. An unstable shadow passed the bedroom doorway and Chester bit down hard on a scream. He turned and examined his newly-built barrier, knowing that he did not have the strength to remove it at any great speed. By the time he cleared a way through to the door, whatever was upstairs would be upon him; and the things prowling outside, in the gathering darkness, would be waiting on the threshold to take him down.

His skull throbbed; things with clawed hands struck at him from within. Outside, in the real world, their corporeal counterparts snickered from the shadows. The lights flickered again, and he cursed the company who supplied his utilities. That quick snapping sound — the same one he'd heard earlier on the phone — began to pursue him down the wide staircase, whatever was making it out of sight for now. He wondered if they'd simply kill him, or if they would use him to supply food, just as they'd used the farmer from the news report. But hadn't the farmer found a way to stop them? For a while at least, until Chester's accident had somehow started it all up again, unleashing whatever force they represented.

Chester hobbled towards the kitchen, looking for a weapon. He grabbed a steak knife from the rack, cutting the palm of his hand on the blade. Blood sprayed the fridge door, so red that it was almost a brand new colour, or at least a shade of an existing colour he had not before encountered. The lights flickered for the last time before going out, and Chester smiled at the inevitability of it all. But it was always dark inside, where the bad things grew and bred, waiting patiently for release. His head felt like it was in the process of swelling, its size increasing to fill the entire room. The sounds inside his skull were also outside, closing in on him.

The telephone rang in the other room, but Chester knew that there was no way through. He listened to it, tempted by its shrill song, wondering if Lucy had changed her mind and wanted to come over.

Then, slowly, he moved to the centre of the room, gripping the knife in both hands, to wait for his house guests to formally present themselves.

NOWHERE PEOPLE

The night seemed to press against my windscreen like a thick fluid as I drove towards the town centre, one eye on the radio recessed into the dashboard as I attempted to tune it to an all-night Jazz and Blues station. Charlie Parker's horn pierced the bubble of stale air inside the cab, and I let myself lean back into the driver's seat, the music washing over me and bringing calm to my mind.

I was tired: dog-tired. As the Beatles once said, it had been a hard day's night. I was at the back end of a ten-hour shift, and my lower back was singing like a chorus of crippled choirboys from being locked into the same position for so long. These suicide shifts were killing me, but it was the only way to make any serious cash in the taxi game. And I needed real money more than ever now: after Jude's birth, Tanya had gone part time to enable her to look after our baby daughter, so I was the only major wage earner in the household.

Streetlights flashed past, blinking like sodium strobes before my weary eyes, and the night folk prowled the avenues looking for mischief. Low rent prostitutes paraded the footpath outside the Mecca bingo hall; tired, overweight beat coppers watched them from shop doorways and ate chips from greasy bunched newspapers. Clubbers and pubbers staggered like somnambulists towards generic fast food outlets, craving empty calories to help them sleep the sleep of the pissed.

The two-way radio in the cab belched static, then Claire's deep growling voice cut in: 'Karl... Karl, where are you? Number 27? Karl, dammit, *come back!*'

I smiled, lifted the plastic mouthpiece from its perch, and told her that I'd be picking up in ten minutes. This seemed to placate her, and she even told me the latest asylum seeker joke that was doing the rounds back at the depot. It was unsurprisingly crude — vulgar, even — and I couldn't be bothered to force a laugh. Claire called me a humourless bastard, then hopped off the line, leaving more of that empty ululating static to take her place.

Two girls who looked far too young to be out this late crossed the road without looking on the zebra crossing that suddenly appeared before me, causing me to slam on the car's brakes. Their thin anaemic faces slowly turned to look at me without really registering my presence, and I glimpsed a profound emptiness in their blank, lustreless eyes. One of them was mechanically pushing pieces of rolled up kebab into her lipstick-smeared mouth; the other was chain-smoking cheap cigarettes. Both of them looked lost, half dead before the age of twenty. I thought of my own newborn daughter, and made a silent promise to myself that she would never end up like that, walking the streets at two a.m., cruising for randy drunks with money in their pockets. In less than an hour these two girls would be bending over in some grimy back alley, or sucking dick in a cheap B&B along the Coast Road. It was just too damned depressing. I felt ice lock around my heart in a sculpted fist.

The girls reached the other side of the road, and a big Mercedes cruised up to the kerb, the driver leaning out of the side window to whisper sour nothings from behind a cupped hand. The girls smiled dead smiles and climbed into the back seat, too-short skirts riding up over pallid thighs bereft of muscle tone. All that remained on the footpath when the car pulled away was the discarded kebab wrapper and some pale, dry scraps of meat.

There was a huge advertising hoarding stapled to the wall at the corner of Mylton Road and O'Reilly Street, selling rampant consumers some new brand of alcopop. Graffiti had been daubed across it in thick red dripping lines; I glanced at the slogan as I drove past it.

Arseylum seekers out! Kill em all!

The viciously droll message was unequivocal, fuelled by impotent rage and directionless tabloid-driven jingoism. The hatred behind the words was terrifying, bland and unfocused; ready to turn on anyone different from what was considered the norm. The people who had written the words operated under the assumption that all immigrants were money grabbing scam artists, even the honest ones. It was at once sickening and heart-breaking.

I thought of Jude once more, fearing for her future. I prayed that I was strong enough to educate her to the dangers of such narrow, uninformed thinking. Hoped that I was man enough for the daunting task that lay ahead. It dawned on me yet again that raising a child was the most difficult and risky undertaking of all: if you screwed it up, you were just adding to the dumb herd, producing another mindless follower. The enormity of it all made me want to stop the car and run into the night, screaming until my throat burned. But I drove on, heading towards my last pick-up of this harrowing shift. My final few quid before going home to flop lifelessly into bed alongside my sleeping wife.

The man was waiting by the kerb outside the Pound Shop when I drew up, shifting his weight from one foot to the other. He seemed nervous, but I assumed that he was just riled at me for being late. He lifted a small brown hand and twitched a little half smile as I stopped the car, then jumped into the back seat, slamming the door behind him as if in an attempt to keep out the night.

'Sorry I'm late, pal. Bit of confusion back at base camp.'

'S'okay, my friend. No problem.' His accent was certainly foreign, but I couldn't place where in the world he could be from. Asia? The Far East? My ignorance of such things truly knows no bounds.

'Where to, boss?'

'Wishwell, please. Palm Tree Way.

Shit. I could've done without a trip to that part of town at this hour. Wishwell was the worst estate in the borough, and the vermin who were housed there would still be up and about, fighting with each other, playing loud music on stolen stereos, smoking weed and drinking illegally imported French booze.

'Good night out?' I asked, making small-talk.

'No, no. I been working. Cleaning offices. I go home now, tend to family. Sleep.'

So he worked the graveyard shift cleaning town centre offices: doing the jobs nobody else would do, just like so many other immigrants in this country. Oiling the hidden wheels of commerce. Paid shitty wages under the counter — tax-free, but with no additional benefits — just to enable him to feed and clothe his family. This hard-working man was exactly the type of person the graffiti on the hoarding had been aimed at:: a man just trying to get by, to do right by his family. I had more in common with him than I did the scum who had painted the vitriol. I pitied him for living in Wishwell, but it was probably the only housing the council had offered.

'Tough shift, eh?' I glanced at him in the rear-view mirror: small face, ever-blinking eyes, creased brown skin.

'Yes, mister. Just like you, I work hard to make something of myself and my family.'

I took the quick route in an effort to save him a quid on the fare- down by the river, past the dark and abandoned shipyard and the flat-roofed clothing warehouses. The man had lapsed into silence. He sat staring out of the side window with those nervous blinking eyes, his thoughtful features bathed in a wash of sodium light from the lamps that lined the kerb along the riverbank. I wondered again where he had come from, what he had given up to come here and feel safe. But was he really safe? I didn't think so. Persecution comes in many forms.

I dropped him at the outskirts of Wishwell, refusing his offer of a tip and bidding him goodnight. He smiled at me, shook my hand and wished my family well. I watched him as he darted across the road, ducking into a narrow alley lined with battered green wheelybins behind a low block of flats. Tom Waits croaked near-tunelessly from the radio, and I reached down to let off the handbrake.

Long shadows detached themselves from some ragged bushes that overhung the mouth of the alley, slow-moving but purposeful: three stooped figures, nothing more than dense silhouettes, drifted into the alley, following the man who'd just left my car.

There was something not quite right about the figures, and my internal alarm bell started ringing. They moved clumsily, without natural rhythm, and their limbs looked too slack, as if lacking any proper working joints. I opened the car door, set my foot on the kerb. Listened. But there was only silence, underlain by the dry rustling of dead leaves and empty crisp packets in the gutters, and the usual distant estate sounds of bass-heavy dance music, crying kids, shouting spouses.

I waited for roughly thirty seconds, and when nothing happened I closed the door and drove off into the night towards a promise of warmth and safety that could only be realised when at last I curled into my sleeping wife's soft and welcoming back.

It was only when I saw the television news two days later that I realised I'd been expecting the report. A local asylum seeker, Jalal al-hakim, from Iraq, had gone missing. He had last been seen leaving the city centre offices he cleaned as part of a five-man crew at one-thirty a.m. on Saturday morning. Police were treating his disappearance as suspicious; Mister al-hakim had only been in England for eight months, after fleeing persecution and torture in his own country. He was an outgoing, friendly family man, liked by both his workmates and his employers, and had no known enemies.

Al-hakim's face flashed up at me from the screen. It was a recent photograph, probably taken by his wife, in which he played with his two young daughters. He was laughing; he looked happy.

But still a shadow seemed to loom over his small frame, shading his features.

My insides churned as if I had an ulcer, and my skin prickled as if stung by nettles. I had been the last person to see this man before he'd vanished; I was a potential witness. So I rang the police without finishing my morning coffee and told them what little I knew, agreeing to go down to the station to make a statement later that morning. But still my conscience wasn't clear: I had driven away after watching those shambling figures follow him down the alley. I felt ashamed, cowardly in an almost abstract kind of way- and desperate to make amends.

I left the house without telling Tanya about what had happened. She couldn't help but notice my reticence, along with the fact that I was more withdrawn than usual, and stared a silent question at me as I kissed Jude goodbye. I shook my head, smiled sadly. She brushed her dry lips against my forehead, blew hot stale morning-breathe against my hairline, winked at me as I drew away and opened the front door.

I went to the police station in my lunch hour, not expecting much and receiving even less than that. It was fruitless. I informed a disinterested uniformed officer of what had happened that night, and about the shadowy figures I'd seen slinking into the alley; then I left, feeling utterly disillusioned. Nobody cared about these people, not the public, the police, or the politicians. All they were was an election tool, a way of faking interest in the community. Local councillors would bleat on about asylum seekers and their attendant problems all day long, but when it came to caring — actually *doing something* — they suddenly clammed up and found some more pressing business. It seemed that nobody wanted to get their hands dirty.

There was more graffiti visible on the flyover abutment behind the High Street on my way back to the depot:

Get shot of immigrint shit!

Charming. And these people thought they were so much better

than everyone else? They couldn't even spell in their own language, while the people they despised so much could speak it if not better then certainly more politely than these restless natives.

By the time I got back to the depot Claire was on a break. She was pouring herself a coffee as I walked in, and made me one with an air of faked irritation so I didn't feel like I was getting special treatment. We sat at the chipped Formica table in the cramped office at the rear of the tiny building, and I told her about my visit to the police station.

'Are you really that surprised?' she asked me in a tone of mock incredulity, that broken glass growl of hers coming from somewhere down near her boots. 'C'mon, Karl, nobody gives a shit about anybody these days. It's dog eat dog out there, and if you aren't a consumer you just get consumed.' She sipped at the awful coffee, her large bland face forming a grimace around the rim of the mug.

'I s'ppose you're right,' I relented, then blew on my own drink, watching with a faint nausea as the skin that the milk had formed on its surface rippled like an oil slick on a park pond. 'I was just hoping for more, y'know?'

'And that's what I like about you: you're different. You give a shit. But don't let it go to your head, because I'll deny ever saying it if it comes out.' She smiled one of her rare sunny-day smiles, then went back to the coffee. I felt numb, empty. Ghost-like.

'Anyway,' said Claire, disrupting my bleak thoughts and attempting to change the subject. 'You heard the latest?'

I hadn't, but knew that I was about to; Claire was the woman to see if you wanted to know what was going on in Scarbridge. She was better than the local news — more up-to-date, and her sources never failed her.

'Which is what?' I asked, wondering if I'd soon regret it.

'Well, it seems that about four months ago half a dozen corpses went missing from the town morgue. Those kids who died from smoke inhalation in that warehouse fire down by the old Dock Road... the silly sods who set it alight while they were trying to rob it? Them. Their bodies. Stolen.'

I glanced up at her, looking for any sign that this was one of her morbid little jokes. Her face was rigid, blank; she was telling the truth.

'Fuck,' I said quietly, placing my mug on the scarred tabletop. 'Some people will steal anything.'

She smiled; a sad, tired expression. 'It was all hushed up by the authorities, of course. Too embarrassing to let into the public domain. People are finding out though; they always do. Nothing stays buried for very long round here. Someone spoke to someone else after a few too many pints, and the news is breaking out like little fires all round the estates. Just like always.'

Four months ago. Just about the same time that the attacks on immigrants had begun: foreign families being burned out of their low rent council housing, kids spat on at school, a pregnant woman pelted with fruit in the local supermarket, one or two people even going missing, just like al-hakim... there had even been a picket line outside one of the town's three primary schools, the parents in the area refusing to allow a couple of Turkish children into the building. One of their fathers had been hospitalised when someone had thrown an engineering brick at his head. It was all so wrong... such a fucking mess.

I wondered if the incidents were linked: whether some right wing group was about to implicate the immigrant community in the theft of those boy's bodies, laying claims to all kinds of voodoo and necrophilia. Breeding even more fear. More violence.

I didn't want to think about where it all might end.

The chill early hours again; midweek in Scarbridge, when all the smart folk are tucked up in their beds, wrapped in sleeping yoga poses around their loved ones. I was returning to the depot from a drop-off in Newcastle — a nice little earner — and decided on impulse to take a detour.

The urge to return to Wishwell came upon me unannounced. Now, with the aid of hindsight, I can put it down to shame, guilt, the need to do something — to do anything. I didn't know what I would do when I got there, but I did know that I had to go back to the mouth of that alley. To inspect the place where I'd dropped off al-hakim for his final truncated journey home.

Winter was closing in like a gloved hand around a warm neck, choking the life out of the world: trees had shed their blossoms long ago, the sky looked brittle as a sheet of glass, and a sharp chill had crept into the air. Yet still I saw young women dressed in nothing more than artfully placed scraps of wispy material and tottering about on four-inch heels, displaying their goose pimples to whoever cared to look. I shook my head in amazement at these people. Once more, I vowed that my child would be raised differently, brought up with intelligence and thought for the future.

Wishwell dominated the skyline to the east, three and a half miles out of town, it's run down tower blocks blocking out the stars. The four central ragged concrete towers were surrounded by a maze of estate blocks — cramped terraced houses, cheap purpose-built flats: the estate was a riot of contrasting architectural styles, and had been continually added to since the early 1960s. I drove to the perimeter of the estate and parked up by the alley; I turned off the radio and sat in silence behind the wheel, remembering those lumbering loose-limbed figures and their odd disjointed movements. How they'd seemed to detach themselves from the darkness like smoke.

Was there really some extremist neo-fascist group operating out of Wishwell? Some militant offshoot of one of the local right wing political parties, whose aim was to clear the immigrant population out of the district, starting with this grubby, downtrodden estate? The thought terrified me, but made complete sense. There had been an intense paranoia and distrust of the asylum seekers who had been shipped into the area for quite some time now, and such reactionary groups feed off negative emotions like hyenas at a rotting cadaver.

I left the car, making sure I locked it up, and headed towards the black maw of the alley. Straggly bushes, like clasping skeletal fingers, had stretched across the entrance, forming a natural barrier that I was forced to duck beneath. It was dark in there, the solitary streetlamp shedding no light. Had it been sabotaged, or was I just tapping into that vein of paranoia and distrust? I stepped gently along the length of the alley, expecting dark shapes to jump out in front of me, their slack limbs waving at me, blanched hands grabbing for my throat.

But I reached the other end without incident, and found myself in a small square surrounded by shabby box-like cluster homes that had probably been grafted onto the estate in the mid 1970s. I registered movement at the periphery of my vision, and spun around to face whatever had caused it; a dark blur slipped away into another narrow alley, followed by two more. It was them, the same lurching figures I'd seen that night.

I followed, keeping to the edge of the square, hugging the rough outlines of privet bushes and lopsided garden walls. The figures were turning right at the other end of the alley, and I waited until they were out of sight before following any further. My heart beat double-time and my mouth went very dry; I felt afraid yet exhilarated. *I was doing something.*

I stalked the men through the estate - I could now tell that they were male by the clothing that I glimpsed beneath the muted orange glow cast by the few working sodium lights: hooded sweatshirts, baseball caps, gaudy tracksuits. They shambled through labyrinthine passages and beneath arched stone walkways, never speaking, not even glancing at one another. I treaded oh so softly, but still the crumbling concrete beneath my feet seemed to mock me: shifting like tectonic plates as I walked and crunching loudly in the heavy silence of deep night. The men didn't hear me; the forces of good seemed to be on my side.

The vast night sky pressed down on me like a huge sheet of black ice, threatening to trap me in the moment until I could be discovered shivering in the pale dawn. Stars blinked out one by one, like heavenly lamps being switched off. The men entered a boxy flat somewhere near the heart of the estate, not far from those glowering grey tower blocks that watched dispassionately from so many broken and boarded windows far above. I hid in a garden in sight of the flat, and waited for inspiration.

Much later I woke without even realising that I'd nodded off. I was cold and my lips were beginning to chap. The estate was in total darkness, and I estimated the time to be well into the ungodly early hours. The sky was still pitch-black, but the stars had turned themselves back on. I let go of the hedge that I'd been cuddling, and climbed over the low garden wall, making no sound and feeling justifiably proud of my stealth. Not once did I stop to ask myself what I was doing; I didn't even pause to think of what might happen to Tanya and Jude if any foul deed befell me. I was focused, determined to do what was right.

I inched across to the building the men had entered. It was a ground floor flat, with dirty net curtains barely visible through the crudely whitewashed windows. The small front garden was weed-choked and littered with empty beer cans, takeaway wrappers, clots of old food. I spotted a thin strip of flagstone walkway along one side of the building, and followed it round to the back. The rear door stood ajar, hanging from rusty hinges. Obviously security wasn't a priority here; but, saying that, they were safe on their own ground, surrounded by their own people, so probably felt no need to lock doors and bolt windows.

I pushed open the door, and waited for the squeal of those hinges. It didn't come; the door swung silently open on a vaporous cloud of dust to reveal a messy galley kitchen that led onto a cluttered hallway with mildewed cardboard boxes stacked against the walls. To the right of this hallway was another door, this one a homemade affair constructed from thick lengths of timber and painted a dull yellow. I rode my luck, expecting this door to be unlocked too. It was, so I opened it.

A steep concrete staircase led down into a fathomless darkness; as I stepped down I briefly questioned my actions then pushed the thought away. I was acting on pure impulse now, shutting off my mind and going with my gut instinct. If I stopped, I would panic: if I panicked, I would bolt — probably drawing attention to my presence in the process. All I needed was one look, a single glimpse into what I knew must be the control room of this sinister organisation. Then I could go to the police armed with proof, and bolstered by the knowledge that I wasn't imagining some convoluted conspiracy and these people actually existed.

The stairs led into a large basement, and it was blacker than night down there; there was no natural illumination, and I doubted that I would find a light switch even if I were foolish enough to try. So I walked into the gloom, so afraid by now that I couldn't halt my momentum, like a man running full-tilt down a very steep incline. I was simply a series of actions, with little thought behind them.

Soon I was lost in the dark, unable to even guess at which direction was out. After a while I began to see shapes form out of the darkness: sketchy figures propped against the seeping black walls. There was no sound in there but that of my own ragged breathing, so I knew that the figures were corpses; immediately after this realisation, I became certain that they were the bodies stolen from the morgue. I slowly counted the outlines that sat slumped against the bowing brickwork: there were six of them. Half a dozen.

My feet slipped on the slimy earthen floor as I advanced further into the room, looking for an object to take away with me as solid evidence. Something crunched loudly underfoot, and I pitched sideways in a clumsy fall. As I went down my right hand pushed against, then slid off some vaguely familiar shape on the floor. My fingers poked into moist holes, and I felt teeth rattle against my wedding ring. A face. There was a face on the floor.

I looked down, unable to help myself. Blind eyes stared back at me, an open mouth yawning emptily into the chill air of the room. It was only then that I realised I'd been walking on the dead all along; mutilated bodies lay in a thick carpet of decay on the basement floor, and as my eyes at last became accustomed to the darkness I realised that not one of them was Caucasian. I was lying on a crust of murdered immigrants.

And that was when I saw al-hakim. Or rather what was left of him. The top half of his torso stood upright amid a heap of severed limbs to my immediate left, his torn face sporting what were obviously teeth marks. Bleached bone showed through like plastic where hungry mouths had scooped out hunks of his wrinkled golden brown cheeks.

I looked again at those six immobile figures that leaned against the wall; at their lurid sports casuals and stained Burberry baseball caps. Something strained at the centre of my mind, a thought that couldn't quite escape its cage. And then they moved. The bodies. All six of them, twitching and jerking like marionettes as they attempted to get to their feet. But still not breathing, not any of them. They were dead; but they moved. Towards me.

It was only then that I managed to regain control of my senses, and ran blindly across the corpse-layered floor, looking for an exit. The figures reached for me as I fled, loose white fingers groping for my living flesh, but I kicked them away, screaming now and not caring who heard. It was only through blind luck that I stumbled upon the stairs, my flailing hands bashing against the chipped concrete and three fingers breaking against the jagged treads. I climbed them in a blind frenzy, wanting only to get out. To be away from that place and those things.

Nobody accosted me on my way back to the car; it was as if I didn't matter, they didn't care what I'd seen because nobody would believe me anyway. I sat behind the wheel for an hour, just waiting and watching the greasy sun struggle up from the eastern rim of the world. If they wanted to silence me, they had only to come for me. As I sat there attempting to set my broken fingers I thought about how easy it would be to steal a few corpses, especially if the authorities were in on it. And I thought about what it might take to raise the resentful dead. To focus all the rage and the bitterness, the hostility and xenophobia that exists at street level to something higher, something darker. Call it urban magic, ghetto voodoo.

If you could bring back the dead you could do anything, even use the undead puppets at your command to cleanse your town, your country, and whip up even more crude bigotry and warped nationalism along the way. Dress them up in England shirts and tracksuit bottoms, and send them out to feast on the foreign invaders, to *consume before we are consumed*.

When I finally started the engine a watercolour dawn was smearing itself across the steel-grey sky. Curtains were opening in windows on the estate- early risers getting ready to face the new day. As I drove back to my family, to my own imperfect little world, I knew that I wouldn't ever fully understand what I'd seen. But what exactly had I seen? Even now, eighteen months later, I cannot be fully sure. But I'm certain that it's still out there, in some form or another, perhaps biding its time in some foetid basement darkness, growing angry and hungry and waiting to be unleashed.

It was only when I arrived home that I realised they — whoever *they* are — had known about me all along. They must have been monitoring me, waiting to see how much I would learn. Someone must have tipped them off about my interest in the disappearance of al-hakim. Perhaps it was Claire, consuming before she herself was consumed by whatever the fuck stalks in darkness. I just don't know. I'm not sure of anything anymore; I don't even know what is real and what exists only in my mind.

The front door was ajar, and as I walked into the hallway my heart stopped beating. I felt dead; as dead as those things that must have come lurching through the twilight towards everything that I held dear.

Tanya was lying face down on the stairs, her left arm stretched out before her as if she'd been reaching towards something upstairs. The nursery. The back of her head was red and matted, the ivory bone of her skull showing through in patches. I didn't turn her over; didn't want to see the expression on her face. I looked up, towards the upstairs landing. The bathroom door had been kicked in; it hung from its hinges like a bomb had gone through it. I felt my body move, taking each stair as if it were a mile high. I knew what I would find when I walked into the nursery, and I wanted to delay the sight as long as I could; forever, if that was possible.

Tears streaked my face, but my throat was too constricted to release any sound. I didn't want to know, didn't want to see, but still I had to ascend and acknowledge what had happened. As I stepped onto the landing carpet, I imagined Tanya moving behind me, raising her head and opening her mouth to reveal a gaping darkness at the centre of her. Lifting herself to her feet and shambling up after me.

But that didn't happen; not yet. Hopefully, it never will.

By the time the police found me cradling Jude's cold, cold body in my warm hands, the tears had finally stopped. The world spun around me like some mad, gaudy carousel, and I could sense things hiding in the shadows of the world. I looked up at the uniformed officers, and had a vague recollection of summoning them with the mobile phone that now lay on the floor under Jude's crib. I looked at my daughter's pale face, smiled at her and wished her pleasant dreams and prayed to God that her sleep would last forever.

I told the police officers about the house in Wishwell — of course I did; but it was no use. They didn't see what I had. The apocalypse in the cellar was still there; although nothing else remained but the images in my mind. Their colleagues had probably been there first, hastily shepherding those unbreathing things into the back of a van and relocating them to somewhere else in the depths of the estate.

I didn't do it: I didn't kill all of those people. But nobody will believe me, not the police, the psychologists, or the friends that have deserted me since my arrest. I miss my family, my babies. They would have believed me.

And somewhere out there — in the shithole squalor of a broken-down housing estate — it's still happening. I read the newspapers with interest, specifically the stories of attacks on foreigners. Last week, an Asian child went missing. The week before that, it was a Serbian mother of three. It's started again.

It's getting dark outside, and nights are the worst. That's when I hear uneven shuffling footsteps in the corridor outside my cell, and hear my name whispered, as if by the wind.

FAMILY FISHING

When I was twelve years old my parents went through a rocky patch in their relationship. There were fights, silences, total communication breakdown. So they decided it best that I stay with my Grandad one weekend late in the summer, to give them the space to sort things out between them; to mend the cracks that had suddenly opened up in the formerly smooth wall of their marriage.

I had no firm evidence, but somehow felt that I might be the cause of much of this strife. I was self-aware enough to realise that my behaviour was at the very least erratic — and possibly even bordering on the antisocial. I was afraid of becoming what used to be called a "problem child" but these days is merely an average teenager.

Dad dropped me off at Grandad's place late that Friday afternoon, his long face stern and pale and twitching under the skin as if a swarm of butterflies was flapping around inside his balding head.

"Be good, Dan," he said to me before driving away in the big old red Renault. He kissed me lightly on the cheek before climbing quickly into the car, and didn't once look back as the dusty distance swallowed him.

Grandad stood in the doorway of his big old crumbling

detached house; he and dad hadn't even spoken. Just nodded silently to each other, as if passing and receiving some mysterious unspoken message.

"Come on, boy. Let's get you settled," he said in his deep, grating voice that sounded like he washed out his mouth with a cheese grater. Then he stood to one side and pushed open the door with a gnarled oak hand.

I glanced back along the unmade road that led to the distant motorway, and eventually to home, and then reluctantly went inside.

My grandparents had lived in that isolated house all their married lives, and even after grandma died of cancer when I was still in nappies Grandad refused to sell it. Even though the place was far too big for him, with too many empty rooms, he wanted to remain there until he died. Until that day came, he haunted the house like a ghost, pacing through the rooms and hallways and reliving old memories.

The house was located five miles outside of a small North Yorkshire village called Fell, and the closest neighbour was about a mile away. The surrounding countryside was beautiful, but bleak. Grandad had always cherished that desolate aspect: it was in his nature.

I followed the slightly stooping but still substantial figure of the old fellow along the gloomy hall and into the cluttered living room. The walls were hung with dark oil paintings — spooky landscapes and dour, staring portraits — and little piles of ancient paperback books lined the blistered skirting. Grandad didn't own a TV; there was a radio in the kitchen, but that was his only concession to modern communications. The old man preferred to read.

"I've made up a bed for you in the small room," he said, glaring at me as if I was an unwelcome guest. "Other than that, you have the run of the house until suppertime." Then he left the room, and short a while later I heard the muted gabbling of the radio and the clattering of pots and plates.

The small room. The term was actually something a

contradiction: every room in the place was huge, the one I'd been allocated was simply the least spacious.

I tiptoed back out into the hall, those unfriendly portraits watching my back intently as I tried hard not to make a sound to disturb them.

The stairs loomed above me, shadows dancing across the thin treads like small questing creatures. Directly above, on the wide landing, stood the upstairs bathroom; a place so damp and mildewed that even granddad no longer used it. The main bathroom was downstairs, adjoining the kitchen, where he was singing quietly to himself and preparing some hand-me-down family recipe too rich for the limited tastes of a developing pubescent boy.

A thin, bulb-headed hat stand that stood by the door was a bulky figure bowing towards me as I began to climb the stairs, and those capering shadows scattered beneath the soles of my descending feet. Darkness hung heavy, like a vapour, and I attempted to shrug off the cloying atmosphere of gloom.

The stairs creaked loudly under my thin feet, and when I grabbed the ancient timber handrail it wobbled dangerously. I couldn't imagine Grandad coming down here in the night and the darkness to take a pee; it was unbelievable that he hadn't fallen to his death on this decrepit staircase.

I turned right at the top, heading towards the small room. My plan was to inspect my bedchamber, and then nose about in the other rooms on that floor. Like my father, Grandad was a hoarder, and there were always treasures to be found tucked away in the corners of this house: armless shop window mannequins, battalions of lead soldiers, rusty bicycle frames, arcane gardening tools and instruments for mending clothes and shoes... the place hadn't been cleaned out for decades, and even then I knew that some of those heirlooms might be worth a small fortune if sold as antiques.

The small room lay at the far end of the landing, to the right of the small stained glass window that never seemed to let in any light from the front aspect of the building. I approached softly, aware of the sound of old boards, and opened the door. Grandad had done a good job; the room was actually quite light due to a large table lamp that was positioned next to the bed, and it looked like he'd changed the tatty old bedding for a modern quilt.

Closing the door behind me, I unpacked my rucksack and laid out my clothes for the morning. I'd been told to bring along a pair of old jeans, a warm sweater, and some Wellington boots, as we were going fishing early Saturday afternoon. I'd never known that Grandad was a fisherman, but it didn't surprise me. He seemed to have tried his hand at most things during his long and eventful life.

The same books that dominated the rest of the house were also present in the room: stacked on wall-mounted shelves, piled against the pitted walls, and stuffed into the top of the wardrobe. I was something of a voracious reader myself, but the titles of the books that I inspected put me off ever attempting to read any. There were volumes of esoteric medical, anthropological and natural history encyclopaedias; heavy books of quotations; masses and masses of poetry. My horizons stretched as far as the odd Stephen King or James Herbert novel, and even most of what I read within those giddy pages was too adult for me to fully understand.

I left the small room and poked my head around the door of the other first floor bedrooms. The most interesting thing that I could find was what I recognised to be a battered ouija board, most of the letters that were printed upon its creased cardboard surface faded to indistinct and wholly indecipherable markings.

"Supper's ready!"

Grandad's voice boomed up the dark stairwell, and filled the empty spaces of the house. Twitching in shock, I left the room that I was in and ran down the stairs, the smell of something hot and spicy assailing my nostrils.

The stew we shared was too plentiful, and its ingredients far too stodgy for that late an hour, so I went to bed with a heavy stomach and a sense of being too full to sleep. But I did sleep, and it was dreamless for the most part, but accompanied by the fear that my parents wouldn't be able to settle their differences, and I'd be consigned to stay here forever; or at least until I was grown up and able to leave of my own free will.

I have a faint memory of Grandad entering my room in the darkness, and placing a cool hand on my brow. I think that I may have been tossing and turning in my sleep, fighting imaginary demons, and the words that he spoke came to me through a miasma of conflicting emotions.

"Get some rest, boy. We're going fishing the morrow."

And then he was gone, and the shadows were closing in.

Morning arrived with the smell of frying bacon. In those days a fried breakfast was still considered part of a healthy diet, and my family had always prided themselves on cooking the best. Huge strips of crispy bacon, delicately prepared scrambled eggs, pork sausages fatter than a baby's arm, and golden bread that had been fried in the juices.

I dressed in my warm clothes and went downstairs to eat; Grandad was already serving up, and had on a thick roll-neck jumper that made him look a little like a ship's captain.

"Eat up, boy. You'll need the energy today."

I sat at the table in the kitchen, and wondered how I'd get through such a huge portion of food. Then, magically, my plate was clear and I thought that I could perhaps squeeze in another of those sausages before my plate was taken away.

At home I'd be pressured by my mother to clean my teeth, wash my face and neck, brush my hair, but Grandad lived his life by different rules. In Grandad's house I was an individual —a man or thereabouts - and could be trusted to do my own thing without being constantly prompted.

"You about ready?" he asked, clearing the table.

"Yes. Just about."

"Good," he said, his eyes coming to rest upon me. I saw a light in them that might have been love, and then it died as quickly and mysteriously as it had flared into being. A sad smile hung on the old man's lips, and then he turned away. "Today we make a man of you," he said. And I didn't have a clue what he meant.

Later, motoring along uneven country roads in his open-backed truck, Grandad broke the silence and told me something that I didn't really expect.

"Back when your dad was your age, I took him fishing too. Same place, same kind of overcast weather."

"Really?" I asked, welcoming any stories of my dad as a boy.

"Aye, it's sort of a family tradition. Like living in that old house. Y'see, in our family the women always die first, and we men folk stay in that big old house to welcome in the new ones that get born. Tradition, boy: it's important. When your mam dies, your dad'll move in there, long after I've gone. I expect you'll do the same, when it's your time."

This was the most I'd heard him say since I'd arrived the day before; the most I'd ever heard him say. He had a nice voice - a storyteller's voice. I liked it when he spoke, even if sometimes the subject matter seemed to go over my head.

We drove for what seemed like hours, granddad piping up with little homilies and pointing out anything of interest we might pass along the way — the pond in which he'd almost drowned as a boy, the clump of trees where he'd smoked his first cigarette, the barn where he'd lost his virginity to some local lass named Molly Malloy. It was a good time, a comfortable journey, and my lumbering and featureless fears from the night before were largely forgotten.

I hadn't spent much time with Grandad over the years, but he seemed to be warming to me with each passing minute. Treating me almost as an equal. He even offered me a tug off one of his cigars, which made me cough until my eyes ached. He enjoyed that, the old rascal. Probably thought he was teaching me some great lesson of the world.

By late afternoon I was beginning to wonder where this was all leading, and then Grandad finally stopped the truck.

We where at the end of a narrow dirt track that finished in thick foliage. Grandad sat at the wheel and stared into the dense greenery, an unreadable expression crossing his face.

"Where are we?" I asked, afraid of the sudden soundless

atmosphere, and the way that the clouds and the trees blocked out the light.

"Almost there," he answered, still staring through the windscreen.

I sat next to him in silence, not knowing what else to say.

"Come-by, lad. The fishing spot is just up there, through those trees. It's a bit of a hike, but you seem fit enough to handle it." And he climbed out of the truck, heading for the back where he'd packed his stuff.

I followed him like a puppy, filled with uncertainty and trepidation.

Grandad had hauled a big empty potato sack from the back of the truck, and was picking up what looked like a short boat hook as he slung the sack over his broad shoulder.

"Where are the fishing rods, Grandad?" I asked. "The nets? The bait?"

He looked at me and laughed, but there was a sort of heavy weariness in the laughter that made me want to run and hide.

"We have all we need right here, boy. This is our kind of fishing, and we don't require any bait."

When he tramped off towards the huddling trees I assumed that I was meant to follow; I had to take two steps for his every one, but managed to keep up because of the weight of the gear he was carrying.

We walked for an hour, following vague forest trails and new ones that Grandad cleared with his boat hook. The sun was beginning to set by the time we stopped, and the air was turning sooty, as if somewhere nearby there was a fire. Country darkness comes quickly, and early; and when it arrives it is total. I knew that night wasn't too far off, even though these were the long summer days. Sometimes the darkness comes of its own accord, disobeying the laws of the season.

It was like that then. The night was descending like a blade across the sky, and already stars were blinking into existence in the clear and distant heavens.

Soon we came to a tall, rubber-insulated gate set in a high, humming electrified fence. Grandad reached into his pocket, took out a slightly rusted key and opened the gate, letting us inside some kind of compound.

"Fishing spot's through here," he said, gripping my forearm and guiding me across the steel cattle grid that was set in the ground just inside the gate.

We carried on for several more minutes, ducking under some low bushes whose branches trailed across my face like spider's legs, and then Grandad suddenly dropped to his knees, pulling me down with him. He placed his big hand over my mouth, and shook his head. I crouched there in the gathering darkness, unable to move.

"Follow me," he whispered. "And *be quiet!*" Then he took his hand away, and tapped me on the shoulder.

I stayed low to the ground and followed him through the smelly undergrowth, sweat pouring into my eyes and my jeans getting filthy from the loamy earth. I felt like a soldier lost deep behind enemy lines: a man on a mission, with only his wits to aid him.

Then Grandad stopped, and reached behind him to grab my arm; he dragged me up alongside him, and pointed into the clearing that had appeared ahead. Initially I didn't realise what I was looking at, but then the details became clear and I was scared all over again.

There seemed to be some kind of shantytown set up in the clearing, with tiny, hastily-assembled lean-to structures and jerry-built dwellings made from corrugated iron sheets. I saw a few caravans dotted here and there, with their doors hanging off the hinges, and no glass in the window frames. They were jacked up with their axles resting on bricks and rocks, the wheels long since removed.

People were sitting at small fires, or wandering around the clearing. Their faces were filthy, and they were dressed in rags. Malnourished bare-chested children ran in and out of the paltry dwellings, bellies distended by starvation, hair falling out in tufts.

A tall woman with prominent ribs and a deformed left arm was breast feeding a baby outside one of the ruined caravans. I stared at her saggy breasts, feeling my burgeoning sexuality rear its ugly head. I was disgusted to find that I had an erection. Then, when I looked at the woman's face all thoughts of pre-teen lust were forgotten. She was haggard, drawn, barely even there at all. Her eyes were as dead as those of a fish on a slab, and her down-turned mouth revealed stumpy teeth that were black as tar.

None of these shells of people spoke to each other; they seemed too tired, too defeated. It was as if they'd simply given up, and were waiting here to die.

"Let's go fishing," said Grandad, and I suddenly remembered where I was, and who I was with.

He leaped to his feet and charged into the clearing, silent as an assassin, quick as a speeding bullet. He headed straight for a group of young girls who were gathered around one of those pitiful fires warming something in a dented baked bean can on the rocks that surrounded the flame.

There was a pause before any of the bedraggled folk realised that anything was amiss, and then the breastfeeding woman noticed him and began to groan.

All hell broke loose: the tattered people scattered like antelope before an attacking cheetah, fleeing and leaving their belongings, running and wailing incoherently; darting into the cover afforded by the trees. Grandad scampered in a straight line towards the girls, intent on his task- whatever that may be.

He grabbed a small one, and tucked her under his arm. Then he turned, and bellowed at me: "Come on, boy! *Come on!*"

I ran to his side, feeling a strange kind of power as people fled before me.

"What about this one?" yelled Grandad, manhandling the girl onto the ground. She was young — probably about ten years old, perhaps even younger. I stared at her wide frightened eyes, then up at my grandfather. I didn't know what to say.

"Too small," he muttered. "Have to throw her back."

Then he was away, running back into the fray. I saw him grab a lanky woman with dirty black hair and pale blue eyes; he tagged her with the boathook, swinging it so that the point sank into the bare meat of her shoulder. He tugged her towards him. She was screaming hoarsely, strangely, tears gouging clean lines through the layered dirt on her face. And Grandad was laughing, his eyes blazing with a distinctly unhealthy light.

He wrapped her up in the potato sack, trussing the whole package with rope that he pulled out in a neat coil from inside. The woman squirmed quite a bit, but after a few hefty whacks from the boat hook she went still. I could see the sack rising and falling rapidly as she breathed; it's a sight that has stayed with me, haunting my dreams and staining my waking hours.

Back at the truck, Grandad threw her in the back, securing her there with a chain that was attached to a small motorised winch meant for dragging heavy objects. Her breathing was deeper now, and I thought that she might have passed out.

It was only then that I noticed the hooves. Where the woman's legs poked out of the frayed end of the sack, a pair of cloven hooves could be seen in place of human feet. And then it clicked, just like that. They had all had hooves instead of feet: the ones that had fled before Grandad, the little one that he'd cast aside in favour of this older female.

As we drove back to the house full night began to bloom; thick black petals of darkness erupting and spreading across the irrevocably altered landscape. I could hear the woman's hooves skittering in the back of the truck, sense her fear, taste her hatred.

"Our family used to own all this countryside, boy. Long ago, in another time. Your great-great granddaddy was a very rich and famous man. Well respected — so much that a great writer even wrote a book about him, making a story out of his work. He was a scientist, you see; studied genetics. But that was before the government came in and made us sell them everything we had."

I felt him turn his head to look at me as he spoke, but I couldn't face him. Not yet.

"But we still have special *privileges*. License to go where we like, to fish where we want. To continue the family traditions."

He fell silent then, realising that it was too early for me to respond.

When we reached the house he sent me on in ahead of him, and I heard him grunting as he struggled to unload his catch from the truck. I went into the cold living room, and listened as he dragged her up the stairs. She made tiny yelping noises as he coerced her up each step, and Grandad muttered a constant stream of obscenities to her, or perhaps to himself.

After about half an hour he came back down to find me.

I was sitting in an armchair, my arms wrapped around my middle, and shivering. Grandad stood above me, casting me in his shadow.

"Okay, boy," he said. "It's time"

He reached down and took me by the hand, pulled me to my feet, and led me upstairs to the small room. There was a key in the lock, and he turned it and pushed me inside.

"I'm locking you in here with her. By the time I come back for you, you'll be a man. Don't disappoint me, boy. This is your rite of passage, your route to manhood. We've all gone through it, every male of the clan. Now it's your turn."

As the door closed slowly in my face he gave me an exhausted smile.

I turned hesitantly, almost too afraid to face what waited for me inside the room, and couldn't even find an echo of surprise within me when I saw the hoofed woman sitting naked on the bed. Her wrists were clamped together, and another thick metal chain bound her legs to the iron frame. Her hands were clasped tightly in her lap, as if in prayer, and her eyes were downcast, staring at the floor.

At last I allowed myself to admit what I was expected to do. It was horrible, vile; tantamount to rape. I was supposed to enter adulthood by coupling with this poor dumb beast, and thus carry on the proud traditions of my forefathers, the bastards who'd owned this land long before my father was even born. Had he done this? If Grandad was to be believed, they all had. Every man who had been born into the bloodline.

I tried to speak to the woman, to reassure her, but the words wouldn't come. I was mute with horror. Instead I crossed the room towards her. As I got closer I could see that she was silently weeping; and when I put out a hand to wipe away the tears she flinched as if expecting a blow.

"You're safe with me," I said, silently cursing my Grandad, and every male who had been here before him. Damning the family name of Moreau.

"*Shushshshsh…* it's okay," I whispered, caressing her sweaty forehead and pushing damp hair out of her eyes.

She looked up at me at last, those cool pale eyes heating up with a glimmer of something that could have been hope. Chest hitching, throat constricting, she opened her mouth and tried to communicate. The cauterised nub that had once been her tongue flapped mutely in her slack jaw; it had been cut out long ago, perhaps on the day of her birth, rendering her speechless.

That was why none of them had spoken back at the compound. Why they'd just sat in silence, waiting for whoever or whatever came for them.

Shocked and numb and ashamed of who I was, I took her in my arms, felt her trembling warmth against my flesh. I could hold it inside no longer, so I let the rage out in a flood of remorse. I wept and wept until, a long time later, I finally fell asleep in her dirty arms.

Grandad stormed into the room early the next morning, dragging the woman from my bed and carrying her back downstairs. I was unable to read his expression when he looked at me, but was convinced that I had glimpsed pride in his eyes.

As I changed my scruffy clothes I heard the truck pull away outside. A short time later, while I was making coffee in the kitchen, Grandad returned alone. He hadn't been gone long enough for a return journey to the compound. My heart sank and I refused to contemplate what he might have done with the woman. When he entered the kitchen he was breathing heavily and his face was flushed a deep shade of red. He looked like he'd been exerting himself, carrying out some intensely physical task.

I felt like stabbing him with one of his carving knives, or

smashing him over the head with the kettle. Instead, I poured him a coffee and we sat together without speaking until my dad arrived later that morning to take me home.

That weekend was never mentioned again; not by my Grandad on the rare occasions that I saw him afterwards, nor by my dad. And certainly not by myself. The subject, it seemed, was taboo, *verbotten*. So much remained unsaid.

Grandad died five years later, succumbing to a quick and reasonably painless heart attack whilst reading a book on genetics. I wasn't sorry; I felt little, if any, grief.

My mother went not long after, continuing the legacy of the women in our family dying first. Dad was distraught, and moved into the big old house near Fell. He became a hermit, a recluse; didn't even turn up for my graduation from university, or my wedding.

He did, however, surface when my son Teddy was born. The old man made the long drive south when the boy was six months old, bearing gifts and smiles and congratulations. Sarah, my wife, was pleased that the family was together, but I just wanted the grizzled old bastard out of my life for good. I certainly didn't want him anywhere near my son, and after two days of silent pressure he got the message and returned to his house of memories.

Now Teddy is approaching his twelfth year, and my father has started writing to me. Long, rambling letters about tradition and manhood, and anecdotes about when I was a little boy. He even mentioned Grandad in the last missive; and suggested that I let Teddy go and stay with him for a weekend. That he could take the boy fishing, like Grandad did with me.

He even guaranteed that my boy would return to me a man.

Even after all these years I'm afraid to tell him the truth of what went on in the small room that distant summer night when I was twelve years old. It was always assumed that I had done what was expected of me. Become a man. But the truth of it is that I will remain forever a small boy, crying hot tears into the grimy, sweat-stinking breasts of something only partly human - a beast I'd thought existed only in cheap fictions, and whose shabby progenitors had been created long ago in my families own tawdry House of Pain.

Last week I went back there for the first time since that weekend. I told Sarah that I was going to visit my dad. That we were trying to work things out. Instead I took his key and went looking for the compound. The fishing spot. It took some doing, but eventually I found it. A clearing within a dense band of trees and heavy foliage, lean-to shacks and flyblown shelters clustered in little groups. Raggedy, semi-naked figures sitting by waning fires, dragging their chipped hooves on the dusty ground, scratching their mangy hides against the rough-barked trees, or just staring mutely at a purely conceptual space located somewhere beyond the great electrified fence.

Soon the time will come when my son will be summoned to go fishing with his Grandad. Part of me knows exactly what I'll say when that call comes; another, deeper, much younger part of me isn't so sure. Perhaps that's the time when I will truly become a man after all.

SOMETHING IN THE WAY

I

"A first sign of the beginning of understanding is the wish to die."

Franz Kafka

"Many people attest to the existence of snuff films even though no one has ever actually seen one."

D.I. Sebastian Fawkes,
North Yorkshire Police,
Scarbridge Division.

The bar downstairs had closed over an hour ago, sending the drunks and the party people careering off into their own or each other's beds. After the music stopped, the silence seemed deafening to Pierce, and he turned on his radio to fill the gaps. Johnny Cash sang about some unnamed Hurt in his familiar aching voice; Pierce closed his eyes and drifted in someone else's pain for a little while. The darkness behind the lids coiled like snakes; Pierce found the illusion strangely comforting.

Various street sounds filtered through from outside: distant stumbling footsteps, cats fighting over the contents of dustbins outside the takeaway pizza joint, car engines purring along the main road, the intermittent ticking of the traffic lights on the corner, changing up and down through their coloured sequence. Pierce slipped into a light doze, the music and night sounds and serpentine blackness lulling him like a nursery rhyme; his breathing became low and regular and his body relaxed for the first time in days.

Another noise, this one more alien to his ears, arose from outside the window, but he ignored the stealthy slithering and drifted into a light doze. The sound continued, growing closer, whatever produced it getting in the way of Pierce's dreams. It was as if a part of the city itself were reaching out a hand to form an impenetrable barrier around his feelings.

A sudden high-pitched squeal from one of those battling felines pulled him rudely from his slumber and he emerged like a swimmer from the sea; the low slithering sound receded, drawing back into the greater soundtrack of urban life.

He blinked his eyes and clenched his fists, suddenly unaware of his surroundings. When at last he recognised the inside of the cheap room above the down-market bar, he relaxed, but only slightly. He reached out towards the old nightstand, his hand grasping the spiral-bound notebook he kept there, next to a red ballpoint pen. It felt cold and dry, like the skin of a reptile. He pulled it to his chest and clutched it there like a bible, or a treasured thing; and indeed it was treasured.

The book was his lifeline, his mind-map, and his mission. It was all he had left, and to lose it would mean the end of everything he'd ever known.

Pierce got to his feet, running a hand through the coarse hairs on his broad chest. As he walked to the bathroom he felt crumbs and dirt on the soles of his bare feet. How had he come to this? Living in a single dirty room above a pick-up joint in a drab northern town, watching transient couples come and go from the vantage point of his smeared window. A twinge of regret tugged at his stomach, trying to make him remember as he pissed in the dirty toilet bowl and stared at his unshaven face in the mirror above the chipped cistern instead, feeling watched by eyes other than his own from behind the glass.

He didn't want to remember. He didn't want to forget. All he wanted was an answer to it all; any answer would do, and he felt that he was so close to one that he could almost touch it. He glanced back through the doorway at the notebook he'd placed on the bed. The words in that book were his route to that answer, clues to lead him to some sort of revelation. Or were they just the empty doodling of a mad man, straws to be clutched at the wrong end of midnight in a cold bed in a lonely room with nothing to keep him warm but a manufactured sense of purpose?

The radio droned from the side of the bed, some late-night deejay spouting banalities from a studio fifty miles away. Spinning platters of love and heartbreak to soothe the sleepless nights of the lost and the lonely. A voice in the dark who pretended to care, to empathise, but who would climb into his car after his shift and drive home to his wife who waited in their expensive house somewhere in the suburbs. Just another fraud, another talking head exploiting the misery of those who were always left behind.

Pierce flushed the toilet, the sound of the water swirling in the bowl sounding like wet feet slapping against stone in the cramped room. He walked to the window, looked out at the street, and wondered if he had lost his mind. The view outside offered no response, and life carried on around him. Buildings sat in silence and people slept or fucked or masturbated in the dark. Pierce felt like crying, but knew that he would not; his tears had dried up long ago, before he had accepted that life was what happened to others. People like him knew only the faded wallpaper of cheap rented rooms, the sound of rain on dirty windows, the forlorn and pitiful smile of a tired waitress over the breakfast table.

Pierce sat down on the bed, feeling the thin sheets bunch up against his arse as he settled his weight onto the squeaky mattress. He picked up the notebook, handling it with care and affection. He opened it with his eyes closed, savouring the moment. When he looked down at the first page, his heart felt swollen with some unnameable emotion. It was always the same. The words on the page seemed to promise so much, yet reveal so little.

He wondered again if he had lost his mind. Then he read the words one more time.

Is something in the way?

Five words in red ink on the narrow-lined page. A cryptic question that probably meant nothing to the rest of the world's population but had come to mean so much to Pierce. A razor-edged enquiry, a hurtful truism: yes, but oh so much more than that.

A clue.

II

It had begun one Friday night in a little dive of a pub near the Victorian town hall building. Pierce was stood up by a girl he had met a few weeks before, a slight young thing with bottle blonde hair and too much make-up who picked him up in a Dixie Fried Chicken place on Pilgrim Street. She took him home for the night, sharing her body and her bed, and he skulked off early the next morning, not wanting to speak to her again. An empty one-night stand, a cheap fuck after a drunken night; but he telephoned her the next day and arranged to meet up for a drink, feeling particularly alone that evening and desperate to use up some nervous energy.

But the girl didn't arrive for their second date, and he got drunk all over again, necking pint after pint of two-for-one Stella from dirty glasses while loud dance music blared like the soundtrack from a nightmare around him. Some time after ten o'clock, he staggered to the gent's, his guts aching and his head feeling like someone had smashed a chair over it. After vomiting in the toilet, he sat down and lit up a cigarette, fighting the nausea that still raged within him.

That was when he saw it. Amid the vulgar graffiti, the thickly scrawled telephone numbers and promises of deep-throat blowjobs, the dirty jokes and the casual abuse of people he would never know, those five words shone out at him as if they were written in light.

Faded red ink on the back of a battered wooden door. The words had called to him in a way that he couldn't even begin to understand. So he memorised them and stumbled outside to find a taxi home.

The next day Pierce awoke to find those words scrawled on the wall above his head in thick black marker. He'd obviously written them when he'd returned home, drunk and angry and needing something that he could never define. There was an empty vodka bottle on the floor by the door, and the intense pain in his head told him where the contents had gone. The note from Sandra was there, too; lying next to the bottle, heavily creased from where it had been balled-up and smoothed out time and time again. He knew what was written there by heart, and memory didn't make the message any less harsh:

I'll be back in a week, and then we'll talk.
If you have any love left for me in your heart, you'll be here waiting.
If you're gone, I'll take it as goodbye.
After all, there's always something in the way, isn't there?

Sand
x

He'd read that note a hundred times; left a hundred times more, then come crawling back through the door filled with drink and self-loathing and regret. He thought that he still loved her, but it was difficult to tell for sure. Their marriage had become like habit; something that they both went through without thinking, and whose impact barely even registered anymore. The lust and abandon of the past had changed to routine and over-familiarity.

Yet still... still, he knew that there must be a spark of passion hidden deep within them both. Otherwise, one of them would have called it quits a long time ago. Fifteen years was a damned long time, and you couldn't write it off that easily. There *must* be something left to salvage, but it would take a lot of digging to pull it kicking and screaming back up into the light. It was always the same, whenever they were together. However hard they tried to get through the damage, there was just something in the way.

Later that day he bought the notepad and the red pen. Over a liquid lunch in a pub filled with hungry strangers he copied down those words from memory: *Something in the way?*

Writing them down had seemed the most natural thing in the world at the time, but now, thinking back, his motivation was unclear. Perhaps he had sensed some latent power in them, a talismanic force he was willing to follow wherever it may lead. Lying on his narrow bed in that cheap room, he thought that he must have known the words were the first point on a map of the mind; a co-ordinate point, after which many more would follow. Where that map would take him was still unclear, but he was still willing to track the route. And he knew that his life might change forever by doing so.

It was three days later when things took a turn for the bizarre. Sandra still wasn't back, even though her note had promised a brief sojourn. They'd spoken on the phone, but their conversations had been stilted, unsatisfying. Amounting to nothing more than the vocal equivalent of walking on eggshells. She promised that she'd return soon, and that they'd talk, but didn't say when. If he was honest, Pierce was losing interest, the gap in himself widening each day to consume his emotions and leave him feeling empty and washed-out. If Sandra was coming back, she'd better be quick; if she left it too long, he would no longer be there to greet her when she walked through the door.

He was drunk again, and staggering home after being ejected from a nightclub a few miles from his house. Passing a public call box, he decided to ring a taxi. The night was cool, and he was wearing a thin shirt; he'd lost his coat in the club, when he was chasing some girl onto the dance floor.

He fell into the phone box, wincing as his shoulder struck the slowly closing door. The receiver fell from its mounting when his groping hands reached for it, plastic clattering against metal in the narrow space. He groped around in the dark, trying to grasp the handset, but his fingers were clumsy with alcohol.

Then, as a car passed on the road, its headlights illuminating his awkward display, he saw the words written in red ink on a sticker that was pasted to one of the small square windows. It was the same handwriting, he knew it: a sloping, almost artistic hand with stylised little curlicues above the letter "a".

The words were different this time, but just as resonant:

Talk to us and discover what's in the way: 08008675982.

Pierce could barely believe his eyes. The telephone number after the words was like a kiss in the dark from a stranger: frightening, yet exhilarating in a way that made him feel sick in the pit of his stomach. He knew that he would copy down the message even before he was reaching into his jeans back pocket for the notebook and pen. He'd begun to carry them with him wherever he went, in the unconscious hope that something like this would happen. His hands were suddenly steady as he jotted down the words and telephone number. He glanced nervously at the phone, but knew that he could not ring the number tonight. Not here, in this badly lit street somewhere south of nowhere. No, he would ring the number from the safety and comfort of his own home, where he could feel at least partially in control.

III

Two am in the morning, and Pierce sat in his living room, the telephone perched on the coffee table before him. He had been staring at the number on the pad for over an hour, and only now felt ready to dial. He picked up the receiver and punched the numbers into the keypad. The ringtone took so long to sound in his ears that he thought the connection would not be made, or that the number was a fiction. Then the ringing began, sounding muted by distance. After ten rings, he was ready to hang up. His hand tensed as he began to take the receiver from his ear, then there was a sharp clattering noise as someone clumsily picked up on the other end of the line.

"Hello." The cultured male voice he heard was tired, slightly slurred, as if the speaker had just woken from a deep sleep — as he probably had.

"Hi. I... erm... I found your number."

"In a telephone box somewhere in the city? Or on a toilet wall in some shithole boozer along a pissy back street? Or maybe scrawled on a demolished building on some derelict industrial park?"

"All the lonely places."

"I know, my friend. I know. You found the number and just had to call. Something in the words that were with it spoke to you. You want an answer to the question."

"Yes, something like that. Something in the manner... in the way they were written." Pierce no longer felt afraid. The man on the phone sounded tired and friendly and open; it was the way he imagined someone who worked for a suicide hotline might speak. There was trust in that voice, and a bruised kind of dignity. The man sounded... *world-weary*. Yes, that was the clichéd description that sprang to mind.

Then the phone went dead, and Pierce almost screamed.

Frantically he tried the number again, but knew before it happened that the line would ring out and never be answered. Soon it went dead, the automatic cut-off system breaking the connection. All he could hear was a thick wet crackle, like tinfoil being dragged through mud. He replaced the receiver into its cradle and lay down on the sofa. Closed his tired eyes.

Later, wide-eyed in the early hours, he tried to watch one of Sandra's DVDs — a film they'd both enjoyed: a light romantic comedy set in some idealised version of London. After putting the disc into the machine and sitting back with a glass of whisky, he stared at the dark screen.

No matter how hard he tried, Pierce was unable to make out

anything apart from the vaguest suggestion of movement within that slightly reflective gloom: a stirring, coiling motion, like fattened intestinal tracts pulsing, or huge snakes tying knots in themselves. He gave up after several repetitive moments, feeling afraid and slightly nauseous. Sitting before the empty television screen, both TV and DVD player unplugged, he watched the same dim, peristaltic scenes unfolding before his unbelieving eyes until the sun came up and burned the images away.

IV

The following day Pierce walked the streets of Scarbridge in an exhausted daze, ending up in an unfamiliar and quietly threatening district sometime shortly after noon. Starved of ideas, he called into a pub called the Royal Doubloon and ordered a pint of *Starapramen*. The strong Czech lager cooled his throat as he drank, and he felt light-headed after only a single mouthful. The events of the past few days were having a strange effect on him, making him lethargic, thoughtful and lonelier than ever before. His thoughts turned often to Sandra, and how he should probably return home to save his marriage. But the motivation was not there. It was all too tiresome, and he doubted that there was any real love left between them anyway. Loneliness bloomed within and around him like a vast black flower, its odour an overpowering charnel stench. He felt enveloped by his aloneness, and a great weight was pinning him down onto the earth, where other people seemed float above the ground like angels.

Something deep inside — some vague and distinctly parasitic sensation — seemed to enjoy his pain. It was as if he was wallowing in it, feasting on his own turmoil like a beggar at a banquet. He wondered if other people sometimes felt like this, or if there was something profoundly wrong with him at a psychological level. Then he ordered another pint of strong lager, hoping that if he drank enough of them the pain, and his secret enjoyment of it, would fade into the background.

It was just after ten o'clock when the woman approached him.

She was tall, too thin for her build, and wore a lot of make-up on her wide face. Her clothes were tacky and inexpensive catalogue items, and she wore them a size too small to emphasise curves that were barely even there. If he'd been sober, Pierce would have run a mile; as he was pissed and tired and sick of his own company, he welcomed her with a creased smile. It was all the encouragement she needed, and she sat next to him on a low stool.

Drink?" he said.

"G and T," she replied curtly, and attempting a pouting grin. The skin on her face pulled taut, giving her broad features a skull-like appearance.

Pierce finished his lager, then went to the bar and ordered. His feet were uncoordinated and his eyes wouldn't focus properly, so he held onto the backs of chairs as he stood waiting for the drinks. He slopped some of his lager down the front of his jacket on his way back to the table, but the woman didn't seem to notice. She sat and smeared bright red lipstick onto her thin lips, inspecting her handiwork in a small compact mirror.

After another two or three drinks, and some dreary, slurred small talk, the woman invited Pierce back to her place. They took an unlicensed mini cab to a cramped suburban street and the woman unlocked the battered front door to a grubby terraced house. Pierce followed her inside, his mind in a place way beyond paranoia.

"Fifty for straight sex. I do not do anal or roughhouse," said the woman as she walked on kitten heels down a long, bare hallway. He realised for the first time that she had a slight accent: possibly eastern European. *Polish? Czechoslovakian?* He couldn't be sure.

"I… er, yes. That's fine," said Pierce, suddenly grasping the meaning of her words. The house was austere, the walls painted plaster; this was obviously a temporary abode for a working girl. He suddenly wished that he could sober up in an instant, like they did in the movies.

The woman appeared from a doorway, shadowy kitchen appliances lying in wait in the dark room behind her, and grabbed his arm as she headed for the stairs. Her cheap shoes made a loud clip-clopping sound on the bare boards as she led him up onto the first floor landing. The door that led onto the main bedroom was scarred, and looked like someone had recently tried to put a fist through it. The room contained a single bed and nothing more: no pictures on the rough white walls, no carpet on the dirty wooden floor. There weren't even any curtains up at the windows.

Pierce fought the nausea that was rising in his throat, and watched in silence as the woman undressed in a sodium spotlight at the centre of the hollow room. Her arms were skinny, with track marks on the pasty flesh of her forearms, and her small breasts sagged like empty paper bags. When she stepped out of her underwear, he tried to look away, but his gaze was drawn to the shaven area between her legs. Razor rash shone there in blotchy red shrieks beneath the paltry light that bled in through the windows, and her loose belly flopped above like a dead fish.

The woman's lifeless suit of skin, he thought, seemed to slither.

The sex was awkward and dysfunctional. Pierce struggled to maintain an erection, and the woman's poorly choreographed attempts at seduction only made things worse. In the end he faked an orgasm just to get some rest, and threw the empty condom she had provided far into a dark corner where it lay curled up like a dead snail gouged from its shell.

When the woman began to snore loudly and mutter darkly in her sleep he got out of bed, crossed to the grimy window, and looked down at the street below. Litter struggled in the gutter, and a few sparse trees waved gnarly limbs from unkempt patches of gardens. A man with a handheld video camera darted through the tiny gardens, as if caught in the act of filming something he shouldn't.

Pierce felt like throwing up, but he fought and defeated the urge. Sandra's face surfaced in his mind, as if breaking the surface of dark waters, and he strained to push her back down into the gloomy depths; she didn't need to see this.

He padded out onto the landing, looking for the bathroom. When he found it he voided his bladder in the brown-stained bowl, averting his gaze from whatever floated in it. On the mirror to his left, scrawled in thick red marker, was another tantalising question —or was it the same one, simply phrased differently.

What's in the way?

Pierce knew without even having to consider anything else that this was another clue. A fresh point on the compass. Whatever he was searching for was closer than he might think, and the message seemed to be that he should keep on looking, keep on pushing. But what was it he was searching for? That was the million-dollar question, the Golden Fleece, the puzzle wrapped up in an enigma.

The truth was that he really didn't know. He was looking, and that was all. And if he was very lucky he just might find something. Something in the way.

And what of that man with the camera? Had he, in fact, been filming Pierce? Following him and recording his movements on tape? Was this some kind of initiation he was required to experience before deep secrets could be revealed?

He left the prostitute's shabby den without even going back into the bedroom to retrieve his coat. Shame and regret and an inchoate sense of guilt pushed him out of the door and into the dawning day as she shouted clipped foreign words at his back. As he ran along an unfamiliar street, then cut up a cobbled alley and headed for a set of traffic lights on a main road, he wondered what had gone so tragically wrong with his life that he was chasing graffiti messages through darkened streets.

It had set in long before Sandra had left, this ennui, and was probably the main reason that she had done so. Nothing had really interested him for over a year now, and he couldn't pinpoint the reasons why. He was just bored, lonely, disinterested; that was why he was desperately searching for patterns where there were none. It was like trying to catch rain in the palm of your hand when you are thirsty, pointless and sad yet somehow necessary.

He let his body fall against a dirty wall in the alley, his legs buckling beneath him and his body falling heavily onto the rough cobbles. He sat there for a while, head in his hands, heart in his mouth, and prayed for answers to questions that he couldn't even ask. What was wrong with him? Why wasn't it enough? *His marriage, his house, his job, his life.*

Pierce retrieved his notebook from the back pocket of his trousers and scribbled frantically. The words he wrote were meaningless, but the act calmed him enough so that he could gather his thoughts.

Sandra; he thought of her now. Of her face when she had walked out the door: downcast eyes, blank and uncomprehending; tears glistening like slivers of ice on her rounded cheeks; her mouth a slit in the thin pale blur of her face. If he was unable to understand what was happening to him, then how the hell was she supposed to? Mid-life crisis, he thought, the onset of middle age fucking with his emotions, churning him up inside.

On his feet again, he walked to the end of the alley, refusing to look at the walls in search of more arcane messages in thick red scrawls. He hailed a passing mini cab and paid a surly Nigerian fifty pounds to get home, glad of these moments of normality amid the bizarre landscape that his life had become.

The sun rose unenthusiastically through a grubby sky outside his window, smearing its glare across the ash-grey cityscape, and he sat staring at the phone. He had memorised the number, but didn't dare dial it. What if it remained unanswered this time, ringing out into some unknown digital night? Or, perhaps worse still, what if it was answered, and the revelation he sought was uttered, whispered like a dirty secret in a tatty room? What if it wasn't what he needed? What if it was? The fear was all consuming, tearing at him like a pack of ravenous hounds, baring his insides piece by bloody piece. He felt flayed, laid bare beneath a staring sky. But he also felt a faint glimmer of hope, like a guttering candle flame, flickering delicately at the centre of everything that he was.

Pierce struggled up off the sofa, still dressed in yesterday's clothes, the stale smell of unfinished sex clinging to them like a string of dried semen. In his trouser pocket he found a folded sheet of paper. The discovery did not come as a surprise. He unfolded the sheet and read the words printed on one side:

all questions answered.

On the reverse side of the piece of paper was a badly photocopied image of an unnumbered page torn from the Scarbridge A-Z. He slipped it into his notebook, and sat down before making a decision that could potentially change his life.

V

Pierce walked the drowsy streets, following the map to the nearby warehouse district. Early morning joggers and waking street people ignored him as he cut a swathe through their routines; he was like a windblown scrap of litter, passing them by without being registered.

Soon he reached the place, an abandoned factory on the outskirts of a group of residential units with *To Let* signs nailed to stakes outside locked doors. Pierce walked towards the building marked with a large red "X" on the map, and found a corresponding symbol marked on the corrugated steel wall of a temporary office unit. The marking was strangely familiar, yet he was certain that he'd never seen it before. A flattened figure of eight enclosed within a circle, like a deflated representation of something that he should be aware of.

He crumpled up the paper in his fist and let it fall to the ground; a slight wind, low to the ground, blew it away. Pierce reached out a hand and pushed the iron door set into a crooked frame. The door opened easily. He was expected.

Without giving himself time to change his mind, Pierce stepped over the threshold and into a darkness so thick that it felt like cobwebs on his skin. The door closed behind him, swinging silently on oiled hinges, and he was suddenly more lost than he had ever been before.

A light went on ahead of him, too bright; blinding in its intensity. Halogen bulbs set into some sort of mobile wooden framework all attached to a little wheeled cart. A large black man, naked to the waist and sweating profusely, pushed the trolley towards Pierce, a cruel smile on his face. Another man — this one Caucasian, fat, and completely naked, manned a camera that was bolted below the lights. His small, stubby penis jiggled due to the erratic motion of the trolley, and he idly scratched at his balls with the hand that was not fondling the camera's lens.

"Greetings" said a familiar cultured voice — the one Pierce had spoken to over the telephone. And then a tall, thin figure stepped into the light, shadows quivering at his back. "I'm glad that you could join us. Personally, I had high hopes from the start; you seemed like ideal material for what we have in mind. You possess great persistence.

"But everyone must first endure our strict interview and vetting procedure, and also pass certain psychological tests, before moving on to the final stage."

The man was carrying the biggest knife Pierce had ever seen, and its curved blade glistened beneath the attention of so much artificial illumination. The prostitute from yesterday stood behind this third, almost elegant, man; she was dressed in a shiny black bondage suit, with deliberately placed slashes at the breasts and crotch. Her head had been shaved, even the eyebrows removed; the skin there was raw and red, like prepared meat. *"Dobry den,"* she mumbled, smiling through a bright silver zipper that was crudely stitched to her thin lips.

Pierce began to cry.

"There's always something in the way," said the man with the knife, slipping off his heavy overcoat to reveal a clean, white butcher's apron with nothing beneath. "Cutting you off from personal happiness and fulfilment; or interrupting that perfect view; or keeping you from your dreams and goals and aspirations.

"And we have that something right here, where we can use it to our own rather perverse — and very profitable — advantage."

Pierce looked again at the camera, at the startlingly bright lights. "All this... this preparation and skullduggery, just for the sake of *snuff films?*"

"Oh, no," said the calm, neat man. "That's not even the half of it. By the time we've finished with you, you'll be wishing simple snuff was all we had to offer."

He smiled, and it was cold as steel, sharp as the knife clutched so delicately in his manicured fingers.

The darkness behind the man shimmered, and Pierce caught sight of something moving there, something beyond the blackness that gathered at the edges of his vision: a long, fat, coiled presence with far too many thick, ropy erections and moist gaping orifices. Then a shape like a fat snake slithered out of the darkness and wrapped around the cultured man's ankles; he kicked it away, smile still lodged firmly in place on his sharp-angled skull.

Pierce strained to see what was there, waiting for him behind the facade, but he couldn't quite focus... there was something... *something in the way.* Then he realised that was exactly what he'd been looking for — whatever *was* in the way.

The fat man behind the camera giggled boyishly; the muscled black man barked a strange, animal laugh. The gent in the butcher's tabard took the girl by her hand and led her onwards towards their cowering prey. She moved sinuously, like a serpent: all loose joints and rippling muscles beneath her soft and lustreless flesh.

Pierce fell to his knees, too weak to protest; too broken now to fight for whatever scrap of sick, twisted film footage his life had become. Their hands were upon him, stripping him bare, and then he was dragged into that twitching darkness, accompanied by the sound of many hungry mouths opening, of fluids ejaculating prematurely against the cold concrete floor.

The next thing he became aware of was the clamouring attention of scores of tentacle-like appendages, the eager sucking of sticky disc-like growths, and a pain so sharp and exquisite that it could almost be called pleasure. He soon succumbed to the grasping darkness, accepting that whatever was in the way would always be there, blocking his view of a better place. And the camera caught it all, in extreme close-up.

VI

Sleeve notes from an illegal bootleg DVD of an underground horror film called *Something in the Way*, confiscated in a Soho sex shop November 2005:

> *A depressed office worker seeks meaning in his life, and discovers a strange sexual cult operating out of the decrepit warehouse district. Here he finds either the answer to his deepest prayers or the realisation of his worst nightmares.*

> *Crudely captured in jerking hand-held camera techniques, this is an example of guerrilla filmmaking at its most transgressive, uncompromising, and unsettling.*

No official record of this title has been traced, and cast and credit lists are currently unavailable.

> *A horrifically mutilated body found buried and partially burned on a Scarbridge rubbish dump was today identified as that of Martin Pierce, 38, an Office Manager recently diagnosed as suffering from severe depression. Police are investigating Mr. Pierce's death, and a spokesperson admitted that foul play was suspected.*

> *From The Scarbridge Echo*
> *6th March, 2005.*

A STILLNESS IN THE AIR

Darkness. A stillness in the air. Thunder. Wind.

Grant stood just outside the automatic doors, waiting for his senses to adjust to his new surroundings. His ears still felt as if they were stuffed with cotton wool and his left arm was tingling from where it had gone to sleep resting on the arm of the chair. He'd flown business class — an extra sweetener from the newspaper who'd bought his story — and had enjoyed sipping red wine as he travelled from L.A.X. to Leeds/Bradford airport to begin his new life. The fee for telling his story had been huge, but he'd argued that it was necessary to finance this fresh start. Money was no longer a concern.

Thunder rumbled again — or was it just the sound of jet engines raking the sky as another plane took off? The wind caressed his legs, wrapping around his shins like a ragged sheet. He watched the people around him as they moved through the endless set of small routines that made up their lives. Soon he would be one of them, faceless and free; but first he needed to find his hotel and get a good night's sleep.

A short oriental-looking man emerged from a recessed doorway as Grant climbed into the back of a cab at the taxi rank near the exit. The man wore a long, grey overcoat and held a compact digital camera to his face. He snapped off a few shots and then walked away, head down, feet moving quickly across the smooth paving stones as shadows skipped away from him.

Just a tourist, thought Grant. *Nothing more.*

"The Happy Inn," he said to the driver, slamming the door as the cab lurched away from the kerb. Jangly Asian music played quietly on the car stereo; a disembodied voice crackled instructions to other drivers on the two-way radio.

"Cold night," said the driver, his moist brown eyes blinking in the rearview mirror. He was unshaven; his hair was thinning on top. His smile was brittle, something that might break at any minute.

"Yes. Chilly."

The man nodded, as if Grant had made some wise philosophical statement, and then returned his attention to the road. Had Grant noticed a glimmer of recognition in the man's narrowing eyes? It happened all the time, and had been the main reason for his troubles: a simple case of mistaken identity.

Grant had always possessed what his mother had called "one of those faces". Bland, run-of-the-mill, there was nothing about his features that particularly stood out; but he was always being mistaken for someone else, mostly people he did not know, had not even heard of.

There was, of course, the oft-recited story of how, when Grant was a child, his mother had rushed into a store for some cigarettes, leaving him outside in his pram for a matter of seconds. When she returned, there was an old woman bending over the pram, talking to baby Grant. The old woman insisted that the child was her grandson, and demanded to know who Grant's mother was and what she was doing with the boy. It was only when the police arrived that the misunderstanding could be cleared up.

Then there was the time he'd travelled from New York to Boston on a Greyhound bus, and spent half the journey talking to a middle-aged man who swore that Grant was his cousin, Jed from Atlanta. No matter how much Grant assured him otherwise, the man had been unswerving in his belief that they were family.

So many times he had been mistaken for others.

Just one of those faces, the kind easily mistaken for someone else.

Out of habit more than anything else, he kept a copy of the grainy police photofit in his wallet; and when he looked at it now, with the advantage of hindsight, he supposed the shape of the face *was* the same as his, and the eyes held a certain familiar slant. He had not noticed the resemblance at the time, but *someone* had. When armed police had kicked in his door at three in the morning, the shock causing his mother to suffer another massive stroke, he'd been caught entirely by surprise.

"Nearly there," muttered the driver. This time he did not glance at Grant in the mirror. The music faded out, replaced by more of the same. The radio crackled.

They had held him for forty-eight hours in a cramped interrogation room, denying him food or drink, and by the time the error had been admitted and he was allowed to go, his mother was dead. When they finally caught Norris Steele, the Florida construction worker who had killed and mutilated twenty-two women, the focus had finally shifted from Grant and he was allowed to grieve. The press finally left him alone; his life, now in tatters, was his own again.

During the high-profile trial, Grant received a letter from an expensive law firm with an offer to settle out of court for the "inconvenience" caused by his wrongful arrest and subsequent detention. It was a lot of money but Grant's ambulance-chasing lawyer had urged him to hold out for more. Eighteen months later he was a millionaire.

He'd always wanted to visit Yorkshire, the birthplace of his grandfather, so here he was, ready to set up home and blend into the greater mass of humanity and lose himself in glorious anonymity.

Drizzle glazed the windows and when he looked out of the car the darkness seemed to writhe like a mass of blackened muscle. Dour streets of identical back-to-back houses passed by in a blur; the occasional pale face peeked out from a curtained window. Grant's mother had never seen this part of the world, but had always wanted to come to her father's homeland. Grant carried her memory with him, hoping that it might somehow help her see the places she had longed for near the end of her days.

"The Happy Inn," said the driver as he pulled into a sudden left turning, rear tyres skidding on the gravel. The hotel was brightly lit and a group of figures stood outside on the steps smoking and chatting in the rain.

Grant paid the fare and jogged across the forecourt, dodging puddles and holding his small suitcase above his head to keep himself dry. He ignored the faint stirrings on either side of him, in the waist-high conifers flanking the path, and climbed the steps to enter the building. One of the smokers who stood there stared hard at him, an elusive expression flickering across her face; then she looked abruptly away, her eyes once again dull and disinterested.

The hotel lobby was slightly shabby and in need of a coat of paint. Pot plants wilted in the corners and by the entrance to the bar there stood a dilapidated antique coat rack.

"How long will you be staying?" asked the petite receptionist when he checked in. The question filled him with a sudden sense of terror: his mind went blank and all he could think of was all that he'd left behind.

The receptionist's smile faltered; her eyes narrowed with suspicion.

"Possibly as long as two weeks. Until I can get settled in the area."

The girl repositioned her smile and filled in the necessary paperwork.

Upstairs in his room, Grant unpacked his few belongings. The rest of his stuff would be shipped out from L.A. as soon as the house was ready. He had not even seen the property selected for him by the newspaper, only photographs. It was a four-bedroom detached house in a semi rural setting. The kind of place he'd always dreamed of but never expected to be able to afford.

Wind rattled the windows. Rain splattered the glass. When he turned around, Grant thought he saw a thin figure ducking down beneath the plastic sill. He blinked slowly, squeezing his eyes hard. When he opened them again he felt better but still not fully back to normal. It would take time for him to retake possession of his own mind; everything felt out of reach, as if he were separated from himself by a thin sheet of unbreakable glass.

He put away his clothes and lay on the bed, on top of the covers. Pushing off his shoes, he flexed his toes. The ceiling above the bed was chipped and stained. Paintwork peeled like old scabs. Beneath the bright exterior, the hotel was slowly falling apart.

Grant stood and went into the bathroom, turning on the shower. He undressed in the tiny cubicle, listening to the hot water as it spluttered to life. Steam filled the room, erasing his reflection in the mirror. Before it vanished completely, he experienced a surge of almost heartbreaking loss.

He stayed in the shower for over thirty minutes, scrubbing his flesh raw under the hot jet. No matter how much pressure he applied, or how much soap he used, he never felt clean. The stain of all those deaths was upon him, even though he had nothing to do with the crimes. Murder crept up on him, hovering around every corner, loitering at each junction in the road. Rooms filled with dread piled above him, tottering on their feeble foundations.

When he stepped out of the shower his skin was bright red, almost burned. He wiped clean a patch of mirror with the palm of his hand and stared at his face in the glass. He no longer recognised what he saw; the murderer had stolen his features and made them into something monstrous.

Steam churned in the air, as if grasping hands were fighting at its core.

"Leave me alone." The sound of his own voice shocked him, and when he looked into his eyes in the mirror they were empty.

He dressed in silence, after hanging his coat over the mirror on the bedroom wall. He combed his hair as best he could and left the room, heading downstairs for dinner.

Grant made plans as he ate his bland pasta dish. Once he had the keys to the house he would buy new furniture and try to assert what remained of his character and make the place his own. It would be difficult, it would take time; but time was all he had.

The staff floated around the room like surly phantoms, filling wine glasses and coffee cups, taking away plates, bringing in the next course. Grant studied them, watching their repetitive movements. Now that the furore had died down, he could be normal again, just like these people. No one here, in this ancient country, knew his name: his was just another ordinary face passing momentarily through their lives.

Once he'd sold his story and the newspaper ran the feature, he could no longer appear in public back in L.A. Everyone recognised him, and the only thing worse than the constant recognition was the look of pity he saw in people's eyes. Occasionally, that look would be one of fear. Despite the real killer being caught, and even though Grant's name had been cleared unconditionally by the courts, women still looked at him as if he was a monster.

Here, in Yorkshire, he would never have to suffer that look again. He might even find someone, and learn to love in a way that had been denied him back home.

Someone dropped a plate in the kitchen. The sound of breaking china was sharp, invasive. When he looked towards the kitchen door, he glimpsed furtive movement outside a nearby window, like a scribble in the dark night air. Surely the newspaper had not sent a journalist to tail him and file a follow-up story? It was part of the deal his lawyer had brokered that he should be left alone for the rest of his life.

A female voice whispered behind him; the sound of brittle laughter erupted in another part of the room. Paranoia swamped his senses and he got up from the table to leave. Eyes flashed his way as he passed by; a couple stared from across the room.

The newspaper he'd dealt with was an American edition, but that did not mean the story would not appear elsewhere, under another by-line. It was a chance he'd taken on the assumption that not many people outside Los Angeles would be interested in re-hashing the story of a serial killer over two years on, but that chance could always backfire.

He passed his own face several times in a series of mirrors hanging on the wall in the lobby. Each one looked slightly different from the last, as if his image was being recreated or reconfigured in the glass. The suggestion of figures twitched in the air behind him, but they were only visible in the mirror. Whenever he turned his head they danced out of reach, as if toying with him.

Grant had always possessed one of those faces: the type of face that is often mistaken for someone else.

He rode the lift in a state close to despair. Tears threatened to fall but he held them back. He could not look at himself in the mirror behind him, and instead kept his eyes fixed straight ahead, focused on the sealed metal doors.

Back in his room, he locked the door and sat on the bed. His hands fidgeted, nervous energy making him smooth the creases out of the sheets. He tapped his foot on the floor and tried to think positive thoughts. Footsteps sounded in the hall outside, stopping when they reached his door. He sat and listened, wishing that they would walk away, and when they finally did so he felt like calling out to summon them back.

A mint under the pillow, a bible in the drawer by the bed: everywhere they were small reminders of a reality he was striving to get back to but couldn't quite reach. Tiny touchstones in a world poised constantly on the brink of change.

He stood and approached the full-length mirror, the one at the bottom of the bed. He'd covered it earlier with his coat, and now, reluctantly, he reached out and took the coat away, uncovering once more the clean, unblemished glass.

They stared at him from the bed, twenty-two of them: blue, brown, green eyes; blondes, brunettes, redheads; tall, short, fat, thin.

Both beautiful and ugly, they gazed impassively, all heaped on the mattress in a twisted jigsaw of naked flesh, bloodless wounds gaping like hungry mouths, pale hands open and flexing, yet unable to fight back. They were the dead: the silent victims of the crimes he had never committed, the murders that had bloodied not his hands, but the hands of someone who looked a little bit like him. And behind them, the vague visual echoes of the families and loved ones left behind: the numberless *unspoken* victims who lived on, grieving and forever damaged, in the gaunt shadow of death.

Grant thought he might have been able to leave them all behind in the States, with the journalists and the clamouring public and the awful memories of the killer's blunt hands in a crowded court-room... but he was wrong. They'd followed the man they thought had killed them, haunting the wrong person, seeking vengeance from the wrong source.

Grant had always had one of those faces.

The kind easily mistaken. For someone else.

He turned and went to the window, stared out into the rainy night, wishing that they would leave him alone but also glad that they were here, to keep him company in all the long nights that now stretched ahead of him. Ghost-tears were reflected in the black glass, but when he reached up to touch his face, his cheeks were dry.

And always, outside, a stark reminder, if any were needed, that the storm never really passes:

Darkness. A stillness in the air. Thunder. Wind.

ONCE A MONTH, EVERY MONTH

"I am he that liveth, and was dead; and, behold, I am alive for evermore"
Revelation 1:18

It was the first day of the calendar month.

Max Jessop hated the first of the month. It was the day immediately after pay-day; the day when all the bills were paid electronically, his direct debits automatically clearing money out of the joint account, leaving very little cash-flow to take him up to the end of the month.

And, of course, there were always other debts to be paid.

The first of the month. It was a bad day, all round.

Max swung his wide, muscular legs out of bed and left his wife dozing; she needed her sleep. They all did: light-sleeping Hannah, fifteen year old Mark and bright little Jenny, now in her thirteenth year. His family needed rest on this day above all others. The first of the month.

In the bathroom, he stared at his face in the mirror. There were new lines on his face; grey streaks in his hair that had not been present the last time he'd checked. Max was getting old.

"Get a grip, old man," his voice said from the mirror. "It's just another day, another month."

After bathing his tired body and cleaning his teeth, he went downstairs to prepare breakfast, just as he always did this on this special day. This *day of days*. Mark was already there, sitting at the kitchen table and staring at an empty bowl, a creased cereal packet on the tabletop near his right fist.

Max stood in the doorway, watching. His son had been acting a little strange lately, rebelling. Something — maybe trouble — was brewing.

"I don't want to go through with it, dad," said Mark, eyes still on the bowl, cheeks pale and drawn. "Not this time. Not any more."

Max crossed the room and stood at the sink, trailing a hand across his son's shoulder. He turned on the cold water and filled a glass. Stared at the liquid before taking a sip. Then he filled the kettle and waited for it to boil.

"Coffee?"

"I'm serious, Dad. This time, it isn't going to happen. Not with me. Let them all rot."

The lengthening silence was suddenly filled by the heating element in the kettle; a low, creaking sound that grew louder by the second. Soon the kettle boiled; steam clouded the air between them, and Max blinked tears from his eyes.

"I know it's hard, son. Difficult. For us all. But we have to do it; we made an arrangement, long before you were born. This is what it is to be a grown up — to take on responsibilities. A lot of people are relying on us. They rely on us the first of every month. If we don't do this, a lot of people will suddenly find that life isn't so good anymore."

Mark said nothing. He just stared and stared, but the bowl remained empty.

"Morning, Daddy," said Jenny, flouncing into the room like she didn't have a care in the world. "Is it time yet?"

"Not quite," said Max, trying on a smile and finding that it didn't quite fit.

"Before or after breakfast, honey?" Called Hannah, entering the kitchen behind their daughter, yawning and stretching and rubbing her eyes. She was wearing the robe he'd bought her last Christmas; it made her figure look fuller, her hips wider, more expansive.

"Whatever you want," he said, sitting down opposite Mark.

"Let's have breakfast first," said Jenny. "I never like to die on an empty stomach."

For the first time Max looked at the carving knife. He'd picked it up from the draining board, where it had lain since last night. The blade was dull, a little greasy. Instead of letting it drip-dry, he should have hand-dried it and put it away in the drawer where it belonged.

His family bustled around him, pouring coffee, buttering toast, filling bowls with assorted cereals — even Mark accepted an offering of Ricicles from his sister, meeting her gaze when she leaned in to kiss him briefly on the cheek.

Max felt a deep sense of pride towards his family, and he watched them in silence as they ate and planned the coming day. He toyed with the knife, fingering the blade. He cut his index finger, but the tiny wound did not bleed. He put the tip of the finger in his mouth and sucked, but still no blood came.

Soon it was time.

"You ready?" said Hannah, smiling and adjusting the neckline of her lace nightdress. She jutted out her chin, stretching that luxurious throat.

"Yes, come on, Daddy. Let's get this over with," added Jenny, taking off her terrycloth dressing gown and undoing the top two buttons of the man's shirt — one of his old ones — she always wore for bed.

Mark did not move. Did not speak. He just sat there, awaiting the inevitable.

The basement door opened slowly, a billowing darkness seeping into the kitchen, climbing the wooden staircase and entering the room, infiltrating the family home. Max looked at it; dared it to try something.

He knew that under every house in town there was a pocket of shadow just like it, waiting, biding its time until he stumbled. Willing him to fail in his appointed task so they could engulf the town and its residents, tearing their lives apart. Homes would crumble; businesses would fail; people would fall apart. The dark would be triumphant.

The black mist settled, coming to rest near the floor. It shuddered, making its musty presence felt. It was merely marking its ground, staking its claim. Firing a warning shot.

"Mark?" Max looked at his son, pleading silently with his eyes. "Are you ready?"

The boy pushed out his chair, leaned back his head and glared at the ceiling.

Max got up and walked round behind his son, raised the knife and brought it swiftly, left to right, across his exposed throat. Blood spattered the table with a sound like falling rain, decorating the cereal packets and orange juice carton. Mark slumped forward, his hands skidding across the vinyl tablecloth. He let out a short exhalation of breath, and was still.

Then he went to Jenny, repeating the process. There wasn't as much blood this time, but still enough to make a mess. It would take him hours to clean up afterwards.

When he slashed Hannah's slender neck, she remained upright, her head tilted almost jauntily to one side. Thick blood ran down the front of her chest, washing across her cleavage and pouring between her breasts.

Max sat down and finished his breakfast, used to the sight of all that blood. It was the same thing once a month, every month, and by now the ritual was beginning to feel like second nature.

The darkness retreated down the steps and into the basement; the door slammed shut. It would not gain a foothold this month; he and his family had kept it at bay... just as they'd done for decades, and would do for decades more.

Max drank his coffee and waited. Then he went to the cupboard under the sink and picked up the First Aid box. He took it to the table and placed the needles and the surgical thread in a neat row in front of his family.

The scars would be gone in a few days, and by the time the first of next month arrived, the skin of their throats would be smooth and clean again.

Hannah woke up first, blinking like a newborn into the sunlight. She smiled, her left arm twitching slightly as she threaded a needle.

"Need a hand?" said Max, knowing the answer already.

Hannah shook her head and commenced repairing her wound, pulling the slippery edges together with a practised ease. Her fingers were slick with blood, but her grip was firm. Hannah had been a nurse on the Casualty Ward at Scarbridge General for the past fifteen years, and was considered an expert at the quick, precise patch-up. When the kids eventually came round, she would tend to them too, making long, neat stitches as they talked and laughed and traded insults like any other teenaged brother and sister.

Max put his head in his hands, and thought about what they had done — all of them; the entire town. Thought about why they had made this deal generations ago with the dark that dwelled at the centre of the human heart, and why it was his clan —the first settlers in Scarbridge; the founding fathers - who must make the monthly sacrifices.

Jenny stirred slowly, slapping her lips like a glutton after a hearty meal. Her eyes flickered open, one of the lids sticking in place. She rubbed at it with a steady hand; she was always the strong one, the one who adapted better and faster than the rest. When Max died for real, she would be the one to take over the responsibility. By then she would have her own children, and her resolve would be tested to the hilt.

By the time Mark came back from the dead, breakfast was over and it was time to start the rest of the day.

SAVE US ALL

"Don't you want to be saved?" asked the taller of the two figures. His accent sounded vaguely transatlantic; yet another yank selling himself as the American dream.

"Only from you," I answered, feeling smug and oh-so-clever and more than a little annoyed at the invasion of my treasured privacy.

The odd-looking couple had been waiting for me on the doorstep when I'd arrived home from the supermarket with my weekly shop, standing still as graveyard statues as I traipsed up the weed-strewn concrete footpath. The woman had awkwardly stepped aside to allow me access to my own front door, but the man had simply stood and stared at me, daring me to verbally challenge their unsolicited presence on my property.

If it were not for the way that they were dressed — he in a straight-cut black sports coat and charcoal pants, she in a sensible trouser suit — I would have assumed that they were both of the same mystery gender. They both sported close-cropped hairstyles, and the female didn't seem to be wearing any makeup at all on her greyish cheeks. Both their faces held a certain blankness, a suggestion of something missing. Or something unfinished.

I turned and stood in the doorway, plastic bags waiting at my feet like well-trained dogs, and only then did I feel confident enough to open my mouth and speak. I was eager to retreat inside and away from the early December nightfall.

"And what can I do for you?" I'd asked, not unreasonably I thought.

I was starting to feel a little nervous, slightly ill at ease. After all, what could an old man with a dodgy ticker do against two fit and healthy young folk if they decided to turn nasty?

"Listen, I really don't have time for this," I said then. "I have freezer stuff in these bags and need to get them inside before they start to defrost."

The woman dredged up a smile, the dull skin of her face tightening as if somebody was tugging it from somewhere at the back of her skull. The man just continued to stare.

"So, if you'll excuse me…"

They didn't move a muscle, and I couldn't help but notice that their eyes were glazed, unfocused. They had the look of blind zealots, or drug addicts, on faces that seemed inexpertly rendered in clay rather than flesh.

"If you have any literature — pamphlets, flyers, that kind of thing — I'd be happy to read them."

No response. Apart from those intensely disquieting sketched-on grins.

Too frustrated at this point to be concerned about seeming rude, I began to close the door. The woman suddenly stuck a chunky foot between door and frame, moving quicker that I was able to register. Her face remained unmoved, the creepy smile unaltered.

That was when I felt the first faint butterfly stirrings of fear in my stomach, like the sensation you get when driving a car too fast down a steep incline.

"The Lord Our Saviour is the only one who can close doors on the faithful," she intoned in a squeaky singsong voice. Her lips were pressed at head height in the gap her foot had forced, and they looked moist and squashed against her lower jaw as they curled round the edge of the door. "Only He can turn us away; but He will receive us again, in Heaven."

"Yes, yes. Very nice." I said. "I'm sure he will. Now, goodnight." And I kicked her foot out of the way before slamming the door on their idiot faces, ensuring that I slid the bolt firmly in place before picking up my carrier bags and rushing through into the kitchen at the rear of the building.

The house was cold, the central heating having once again failed to come on at the hour I'd programmed into the defective timer switch. Winters seemed to be growing more harsh as the years advanced; at least when Vera was around we had been able to rely on body heat to warm us while the radiators warmed up.

But my Vera had been dead for three long years and the only way I could see her now was to look at the framed photograph I kept on the mantle above the broken gas fire that I couldn't afford to have repaired.

The picture was a snap taken of my wife on her fiftieth birthday, back when she'd still possessed some of the vigour of her youth. I remember the moment well: she'd been turning her head, smiling at the camera, as she cut the cake I'd had specially made for the day. Two years after the picture was taken, age had caught up with Vera, planting tumours and blood clots in her veins and turning the marrow in her bones to chalk dust.

After putting away my meagre provisions, I washed my hands at the sink. I gazed out of the window and into the small back garden that I tended so obsessively in Vera's honour — when she'd been physically able, she'd loved pruning her roses, weeding the planters, and turning the rich soil.

My eyes came to rest on the unwashed windows of the house that backed on to my own. Bodies shimmered like shapeless masses behind the greyish net curtains, whoever lived there having forgotten to turn on the lights. Or perhaps they were trying to save on electricity. Maybe they were even pensioners like me and could barely afford to pay the council tax never mind criminally high utility bills.

I ghosted back out into the hall, feeling sad and strangely light on my feet, noticing as I did so that the unwelcome cold-callers were still standing outside my front door. I could make out their blurred outlines through the frosted glass; their heads looked stretched and distorted, arms hung far too long, like those of great apes.

They moved even as I observed them, turning away and shuffling back along the garden path and onto the pavement. I entered the living room and watched them as I closed the curtains to keep out the night; they were heading for the stumpy block of council flats opposite. Oh, they'd get more than they'd bargained for there! Surly teens in baseball caps, grubby mothers who swore and chain-smoked and hung around the shopping precinct dressed exactly like their offspring.

These days it is difficult to discern who the real adults are.

I remained where I was, peeping like a nosey housewife through a half-inch gap in the heavy drapes. Three more people appeared from some hidden alley or side street and joined the couple at the kerb, and then the entire loosely knit group approached a door that they seemed to pick at random.

The way the strangers moved was odd, artless, as if they all had trouble bending their limbs. I thought that they resembled the puppets I'd enjoyed seeing perform in seaside Punch and Judy shows as a boy: rudimentary features, slack postures, stiff, arthritic movements.

Suppressing a shiver not entirely caused by the drop in temperature, I moved away from the window. The last thing I saw before closing up the gap was one of the small band of people reaching out a fisted hand to knock on the door.

I made myself a bowl of soup and sat eating it in front of the television. Vera had never allowed me to do that when she'd been around to object, but now I did it just for the company. A televised voice in the house was better than none at all, even if it did belong to some mincing Liverpudlian transvestite on what passed for a quiz show.

The soup was unbearably bland, so I left most of it, setting the bowl down on the low coffee table at the side of my comfy armchair. The table lamp that provided the only illumination in the room flickered a couple of times, then finally settled. There had been a few blackouts over the past months, and I hoped to God that this didn't signal the approach of another.

The older I got the more fearful of the dark I became. It was like regressing to the point in my childhood where I'd been most afraid. Back when I was ten-years-old I'd been scared of everything, but darkness (and the threat of what it concealed) had been the worst, the ultimate terror.

Now I tended to see faces looming in the darkened rooms of my house, and the smeared outlines of heavy bodies swimming like whales through the gloom. Vera had kept me safe from such imaginings, but now her protection was gone.

I got to my feet and turned on the main light, blinking at the sudden transition from dim to too bright. Then I took my dinner dishes through into the kitchen and placed them by the sink, ready for washing in the morning.

There came a sound from the front of the house: a sharp clattering thud, as if something substantial had collided with a front wall of one of the neighbouring buildings.

Stepping slowly and quietly through to the front door, I peered out through the tiny glass spy hole I'd had the son-in-law of the man up the road install immediately after Vera's funeral.

There was a large mob of people gathered outside the entrance to one of the flats across the way. Some sort of commotion seemed to be taking place - a row or disagreement. I could clearly hear raised voices, snatches of angry conversation.

Someone was telling the door-to-door God Squad who'd bothered me earlier to go away — and in no uncertain terms. A burly gentleman with tattooed arms who stood outside gesticulating in a vest and shorts despite the seasonal chill.

I pressed my eye to the glass, straining to make sense of the images given false distance by the distorting fish-eye lens.

Seven or eight figures stood smiling around the shouting man, and in response to his insults and obscenities they all reached slowly towards him with unnaturally long hands that looked to have too many fingers.

A car flashed by on the road between my house and the block

of flats, obstructing the view for perhaps a couple of seconds. Certainly no more than that. By the time the vehicle had passed all was calm; the previously enraged resident now stood in silence, mouth hanging open in such a way that it seemed to be dangling on a faulty hinge.

Then the suddenly taciturn man led the group inside his home, and the door slammed shut on the back of the last one in.

I prised my eyeball away from the peephole and forced myself up to bed, where I slept uneasily, thinking of Vera and how much I missed her company.

The next morning was a Saturday and I slept uncharacteristically late, due mostly to my troubled night's slumber. Rising just after 10am, I washed, dressed, and then cooked an early lunch. My head felt heavy, stuffed with cotton balls; my mouth was dry as old bones and my eyes itched maddeningly.

I locked up the house and decided to take a stroll down by the canal, where bleary-eyed weekend fathers dragged sleepy toddlers into the frosted park and hyperactive dogs took listless owners for brisk jogs along the gritty litter-lined towpath.

Paranoia hung over me like a cloak: glazed eyes watched me from all quarters. The skinny branches of deformed winter-bare trees hid stunted stick figures, and a thin man in a knee-length Macintosh inspected my progress intently from the other side of the canal through a large pair of binoculars.

The cold was nipping like claws, so I truncated my constitutional. Taking a shortcut through the car park behind the bus depot, I made my way back to my safe little suburban haven.

The rest of the day was spent reading Dickens and I just about managed to lose myself in the London of a bygone era, where men wore tops hats and women paraded in huge conical skirts that hid more than a multitude of sins.

By sunset I was feeling edgy, and as the sky turned a deep shade of crimson I checked that all the doors and windows where secured against more than just the cold.

I watched some television with the sound turned down low for a little while, and then unable to resist the temptation for any longer, I twitched aside the living room curtain and looked for signs of what I can only term oddness outside.

Most of the house lights in the street were turned off — except for the ones inside the very flat that the annoying word-spreaders had entered the previous night. I glimpsed movement behind the glass, and occasionally a face would turn to stare in my direction. Although certain that I could not be seen, I turned out the lights and retreated upstairs in hated darkness.

Over the next few hours people left the burly man's dwelling in small groups of two or three, visiting several of the other flats in the same block. Then they progressed along the quiet street, knocking on doors and rapping on darkened windows. Each time a door was opened to them a discussion ensued — sometimes animated, most times not. Each of these exchanges ended in the same way: the visitor would reach out a hand, casually touch the forehead of the other person, and be wordlessly invited inside.

I watched from a first floor window, unsure of what I should do. If I called the police, or any of the other emergency services, what was I supposed to report? A feeling that all was not well? A hunch that the neighbours I barely even spoke to — despite having lived among them for twenty-five years — were being coerced into joining some kind of religious cult?

No. That simply would not do. I was being paranoid again, scared of my own cowering shadow. I hated being old, lacking in any kind of physical strength. Old age meant nothing more to me than fear and regret, and I was being mercilessly eaten alive by demons of my own creation.

So I sat in the dark and spied on them, deathly afraid of what nestled in the dense and silent shadows that gathered inside the room, but far more fearful of what was going on out there, up and down the night-time street.

Yet more figures drifted to the impromptu block party, arriving from points unknown. From other houses, other streets. A few cars and a battered mini-bus even pulled up at the kerb, disgorging even more of the shambling stiff-limbed gatecrashers.

Then, at some point just before one in the morning, something new happened. Something entirely unexpected.

Those inside the shabby flats suddenly spilled out into the street, stealthy and silent as thieves. They lined up and stared at my house, as if they knew that I was watching them. I decided that they probably did.

It was only then that I allowed myself to admit that the entire street had been taken over, and that the only house in the district from which they had been turned away was mine. Every other door stood open; every other heart and hearth laid bare to this strange invasion.

They stepped forward in unison, a slow-marching army of broken dolls. When they reached my low garden wall they swarmed over it, circling the house like crippled scavengers.

I found myself unable to move, unable to scream. The darkness inside the house was closing in on me, and then engulfed me in an instant as the lights I'd left on downstairs suddenly went out.

I did not know what else to do, so I continued my watch.

A single figure was pushed to the front of the gathering on my clipped front lawn, limping and shuffling like an inexpertly animated marionette.

It was an old woman, her shoddily etched features resembling those of my dead wife. It was as if a rough version of Vera's aged face had been stencilled onto the empty head of a department store mannequin. Her thin mouth, small, deep-set eyes, the dark worry lines in her pale brow... all evoked as a graven image so that I might be tempted to follow peacefully wherever they led.

Tears began to stream down my cold, cold cheeks, and I struggled to understand what I was being shown. Then I heard the sound of breaking glass and of clumsy bodies flopping through into the rooms downstairs.

I dearly hoped that whatever was on its way to convert me would do so only after the darkness had swallowed me completely, saving me the horror of seeing my own hastily scribbled face bearing down on me with a dead cartoon smile.

They entered the room one by one, lining up against the wall, lying across the neatly made bed, leaning against the wardrobe. I turned to face them, to embrace what I was about to become. Hand-drawn faces leered from the darkness, thin pencil lips twisting into uncomfortable smiles.

The facsimile of Vera stood among them, not even recognising me as I silently pleaded with her to take me in her arms and soothe away the night terrors, just as she'd done so many times before.

And just as I reached out my thin arms to accept the inevitable, they walked away. Leaving the room quicker than they had entered it, and not even looking back at me as I shuffled pathetically forward on my aching knees to follow.

They had rejected me. For some uncertain reason I was not fit to join their ranks, and they had only broken in to tell me so. A street was chosen, and I had been left behind.

I slid to the floor, as loose and boneless as a rag doll... or a puppet deprived of its strings. When dawn finally arrived I was still there: stiff as marble, still and lifeless as the street outside.

If I wait here long enough they might return, lumbering along the highways and byways, tumbling over motorway safety fences and wading through the shallow and stagnant waters of the old canal.

If I wait here long enough they might return to save me. Just like they saved everyone else.

A BIT OF THE DARK

I

"Nobody heard him and nobody saw,
His is a picture you never could draw,
But he's sure to be present, abroad or at home,
When children are happy and playing alone."

Robert Louis Stephenson,
The Unseen Playmate

Frank Link stood on the slight rise above the busy motorway bypass, surveying the pathetic remains of the place he'd called home for three terrible years of his troubled youth. Tension flared across his shoulders and he was unable to relax his facial muscles out of the scowl they'd twisted into minutes earlier. The sound of the traffic below and behind him did nothing to alter his mood; anger was the dominant emotion and it bounced around inside him like the metal ball in a pinball machine.

Black sheets billowed at the edges of his vision like curtains blowing in a strong breeze, but whenever he turned to look there was nothing there. Just settling dust and the sensation of being watched from afar. It was a feeling he'd grown accustomed to across the years.

Riven Manor was in ruins; and that was exactly the way he liked it. The demolition squad had moved out three days before, and now he could see the place for what it truly was, a flattened pile of old masonry, rotten timber and dark, dark memories.

"Are you okay, honey?" asked his wife, moving close and linking her arm into the crook of his elbow.

"It's dead," he said, meaning more than the building; the dark place inside his heart that Riven Manor had created.

"I know, Frank. The monsters can't get you now."

He turned to her and smiled, tears welling at his eyes. She looked beautiful standing there against the clear afternoon sky, her blonde hair done up in a loose ponytail and her sparkling brown eyes seeing only him and nothing of the crushed but still twitching horrors spread out below. Claire knew little of the terrors he'd experienced as a child, but what she did know horrified her. The treatment Frank and the other boys had received here could not be excused, and Claire was all for suing someone. Anyone.

Frank smiled at her, his thoughts flying sky-high. She was a caring, understanding woman, but it was best if she did not know the full truth of what had happened all those years ago. If he told her, he feared she might never look at him in the same way again.

He'd spent most of his life exorcising the demons of Riven Manor. Writing about them in his novels, feeding them bit by bit into the mincing machine of the film industry by way of screenplays for low budget horror movies, and finally, now that the place had been brought tumbling down, he felt on the verge of some kind of closure.

"Where's the boy?" he said, holding her hand and gently rubbing his thumb along the side of her palm.

"Exploring."

A sharp spur of horror raked along the meat of his mind, drawing old blood. But then he remembered that it was all over, and nothing could happen to his son. The monsters were dead; only bad memories remained.

II

Terry ran along the edge of the pit, looking down at the exposed foundations. A sturdy wooden fence surrounded the area, but he'd managed to enter through a section where two uprights had been pulled apart — possibly by local vandals. The walls inside the compound had been torn down, the roof lay in tatters on the dusty ground, and Terry was amazed that such a huge building could be reduced to so much rubble.

He glanced back up the hill, at his father and mother standing there like biblical statues. He'd been warned to stay back, to keep away from the debris, but no ten year-old boy in creation could ever resist the lure of a building site. Leaping into the shuttered trench, Terry imagined that he was a W.W.II soldier on a mission deep into enemy territory. If he were discovered here, in the ruins of this French hotel, he would be captured and tortured by the dreaded General Heinz Boobyhoff, Nazi scourge of the allied forces!

It was a bright day; the sun was just past its peak. Terry took off his sweater and tied it around his middle, pretending it was an ammo belt. He picked up a stick shaped roughly like a pistol, and held it before him, ready to take down any enemy troops he encountered along the way. Rubble crunched underfoot and he almost twisted his ankle on a fallen door that splintered beneath his weight.

When he saw the boy, Terry was so caught up in his game that he almost ran up behind the lad and clobbered him over the head with his makeshift weapon.

He stopped running, breathing heavily and wondering if the boy had heard his noisy approach. All Terry could see of him was a narrow back and the nape of a thin neck; the boy was sat huddled over something, poking at it with a length of oil-stained copper pipe.

Terry approached with caution. The boy could be a Nazi sympathiser.

"Hello," said the boy without turning around.

"Come and see what I've found."

Terry drew level with the stooped figure, and peered over his shoulder. There was a hole in the ground, about the size of the bathroom window at home, and the boy was pushing stones over the rim and into the darkness below. Terry listened: the stones were taking a long time to drop. The sound they eventually made as they hit bottom sounded faint and incredibly distant.

"My name's Franz," said the boy, turning his head to look up at Terry. "I used to live here."

A solitary cloud chose exactly that moment to cross the sun, darkening the area around he and the boy; Franz's eyes were immediately lost in shadow and his mouth twisted into a strange leering grin. He slowly stood, reaching his full height, and placed a tiny hand on Terry's arm.

Terry tensed; he did not like to be touched - especially not here, in this lonely location, and certainly not by this odd and slightly intimidating fellow. He opened his mouth to say so, but the words got stuck in his throat.

"Will you be my friend?" Franz muttered, blinking like a lizard as the sun came out of hiding.

"*Terry!*" His mother's voice, sounding panic-stricken.

Terry pulled away from Franz, stumbling on the broken bricks, falling sideways and on top of the loose timbers that covered the hole like vertical blinds across a small window.

Then he fell, and nothing seemed the same again.

III

They left the hospital and booked into a cheap hotel, fraught with worry regarding their only son. The doctor had said that Terry was merely suffering from shock; he'd banged his head slightly in the fall, but all he'd have to boast about at school next week was a small swelling above the left ear. Frank bit his nails, worrying a sliver of loose skin on his ring finger. Sometimes being a parent was the most demanding and difficult job in the world.

"He'll be okay. He *is* okay" Claire whispered as they set their things down on the incredibly narrow double bed. There was little furniture in the room apart from the bed, a spindly high-backed chair, two frail-looking bedside cabinets and a battered single wardrobe.

"I know, I know. It's just that…"

"You can't handle him being hurt."

"Yes, that's it." Frank sat down on the rickety wooden chair by the bed, kicking off his muddy shoes. "I hate this feeling of powerlessness. I know he's okay this time, but what about next time? What if he has some kind of major accident or contracts a severe illness?"

"We've been through all this before, Frank. Just because you had an awful childhood doesn't mean that our son will too. You're a fucking great dad; I'm a terrific mother. He'll survive." She smiled, reached out a hand to smooth down his fringe, as if he were the child in question.

"I love you, you know. Just… just remember that. Whatever happens."

"Me too," Claire responded, pulling him down into a deep kiss. "And everything is going to be fine."

They lay on the bed for half an hour, just holding each other. It always made Frank feel more secure to know that his wife kept him tethered to the earth. Sometimes he felt that if she were to release her grip he'd simply float away. Other times he wished she'd just let him go. Images from the latest book ran through his head: he was developing the idea of a creature called the Hugger, something dark and bestial that climbed out of the horror of childhood nightmares to literally *embrace* children to death.

Frank's dark pulp horror stories had been selling well for years, enough that he enjoyed a reasonable income. Film options brought in more money (even though none of his books had actually made it to the screen) and he made a few quid from toiling over other people's film scripts, trying to whip them into shape before the cameras rolled and the budget was spent.

But it wasn't the money that mattered. It was the catharsis.

Frank had been abandoned as a baby, and the authorities had sent him to countless foster homes and hostels before the staff at Riven Manor, the local state-funded orphanage, had finally taken him in. It was a sort of last-stop house, the place where mistakes were routinely sent to be swept under the carpet. Things had been bearable until he was sent there at the age of seven, and he had suffered three years of the most horrific abuse imaginable, both sexual and psychological. He still could not think of those times without coating them in fantasy, easing their passage through his memory adorned with the costume jewellery of imagination. But in his dreams he saw it all as it had really happened. Thankfully, when morning came, he rarely remembered much apart from an unbearable sense of claustrophobia.

Names and faces had been kept from him — his silent abusers entered his room in the dead of night, their features obscured by stocking masks, voices disguised, but dark intentions all-too clear. Frank had adopted fantasy as the only viable method of escape, retreating inside himself when the regular attacks took place. During the day he wrote stories informed by his pain, violent revenge scenarios and fables about abducted children. He became obsessed with Peter Pan and the "Lost Boys"; he wished that he could fly, but the type of belief necessary for such a feat was a luxury he could not afford to risk.

Thankfully, he'd blocked out the details. Therapy was a no-go area for him in case he started to remember. He didn't want that; all he wanted was to forget completely what had been done to him under the tilted roof of Riven Manor.

"That's a serious face," Claire said, sliding her arm out from under him and straddling his tight abdomen. "You have that look in your eyes — the one I don't like."

"The one I get when I'm writing?"

She nodded, climbed off him and walked to the bathroom. "I'll run you a bath," she said, opening the door and disappearing inside. The picture — a bad print of Edvard Munch's *The Scream* —

hanging on the wall to the left of the door wobbled on its nail, threatening to fall. It took a long time to settle, and when it finally did so, Frank could not tear his gaze away from the gaunt figure at its centre.

When his bath was ready Claire stepped outside to hunt for a shop where they could buy a bottle of wine. She was determined that her husband should unwind, and her single-mindedness was nothing short of exhilarating. Frank stripped off his clothes and stood before the bathroom mirror. Steam had clouded the glass, so he swept a hand across it to clear the view, creating a thick dark smear.

For a moment he imagined that he saw the figure of a small boy standing behind him, only the top of a tousled head visible above his right shoulder, small hands rising to tenderly touch the nape of his neck.

The image lasted only a second; it was long enough for him to realise that Claire was right, he was letting Terry's accident get to him. The kid was fine, just a few scratches and a big bruise. They were keeping him in overnight as a cautionary measure because of his age, that was all.

But they way they'd looked at Frank in the hospital had felt like a violation, and the probing questions they asked were like groping fingers inside his head, feeling around the dark places. He understood that if an injured youngster was brought into the Casualty Department alarm bells rang — it was only natural, and actually rather reassuring. But that didn't negate the sense of intrusion that he and Claire had to suffer just to confirm that Terry's injuries weren't the result of parental mistreatment.

The episode had triggered fresh questions in Frank's own mind. Was abuse hereditary, as the so-called experts constantly stated? Was he potentially an abuser of his own issue? Did he have it in him to be the character from his latest book, the despicable and insidious Hugger?

Perhaps that was what the entire project was really about.

He sighed, shook his head. Sometimes Frank found it difficult to differentiate between what was real and what he imagined. His fictions became too much like fact for comfort, and Claire was a martyr to look after him the way she did. She'd lived through her own traumatic childhood, and the way she coped was by looking after her husband and child. Transforming all of her resentment into love and affection. He often envied her ability to do this, and sometimes wished that instead she would react badly to his moods, if only to justify the spiteful thoughts he sometimes entertained about her.

But she didn't. She knew him too well to be sucked into the hungry vortex of his despair.

He climbed into the hot bath, enjoying the scalding sensation up his calves and along the backs of his thighs. As he lay down the bubbles covered his stomach, hiding the scars there from view. They still bothered him, those scars; but all he could remember about their origin was the image of a broken bottle being pressed against his flesh by someone he was supposed to trust.

Frank closed his eyes and let himself be taken away. Within minutes, he was dozing.

IV

Claire paid for the wine and left the shop, feeling like she'd enjoyed a small victory by finding the establishment in such a rundown area of town. The proprietor, a tiny Asian woman with a wispy grey beard, had been about to shut up shop to attend some family function when Claire had pushed open the door to inspect the dusty aisles of out-of-date canned food, rotting vegetables and magazines left over from the previous decade.

After buying the best wine she could find, she climbed into the car and placed the wine on the passenger seat, fastening her seatbelt and preparing to pull away from the kerb. She was worried about Frank; he'd been acting odd for the past week. Sure, he'd been nervous about visiting the site of the orphanage to see the place finally put to rest, but his moods were darker than ever. And what little she'd read of this latest book was much more bleak and violent than his usual stuff.

Terry had looked okay — if a little pale — when they'd left him at the hospital, and the nurse she'd spoken to while Frank was having a panic attack in the toilet had assured her that all their son had suffered was a case of mild shock. Still, it had been a nasty scare, especially when, in the ambulance they'd summoned on Frank's mobile phone, Terry had babbled something about another boy pushing him down the hole.

It was nonsense of course: there'd been no one else on the scene. She and Frank had witnessed the accident at a distance, and Terry had been standing alone, peering into an exposed foundation trench. He'd stumbled backwards, losing his footing in the freshly excavated soil, and simply tumbled onto some boards that had been thrown over a void that led directly into the basement.

Terry had taken harder falls than this one during his first ten years of life; and no doubt he'd live through a lot worse. He was a tough little kid: he took after his mother.

Claire grinned and joined the light evening traffic, heading back to the hotel. She glanced into her rearview mirror, watching the CLOSED sign appear in the shop window, and for a moment had the unsettling feeling that someone had ducked down out of sight on the back seat.

It was getting dark, so she turned on her lights; bands of illumination flooded the road ahead, revealing potholes and discarded litter. Again she experienced the sensation that there was someone behind her — this time, whoever it was had sat up. She looked in the mirror. There was no one there. The bright afterimage of a small boy with dark blonde hair was burned into her retina, like a subliminal image glimpsed between frames in a film.

When she reached the hotel Claire got out of the car and opened the rear door. The back seat was empty; she smiled at her foolish compulsion. Slamming the door, she marched towards the squat, ugly two-storey building, glancing back over her shoulder and through the gathering darkness. A small boy sat behind the wheel of the car, smiling lasciviously.

V

Frank opened his eyes and gasped; water poured into his open mouth, making him cough and choke. God knew how long he'd been asleep, but the bath water was barely lukewarm. It felt like he'd been out for hours. He sat up and stretched from a sitting position, hearing the bones in his back pop like distant gunfire. The pain that flared there was the result of more dimly recalled childhood beatings: yet another grim souvenir of Riven Manor.

He got out of the bath and dried himself down with a surprisingly fluffy hotel towel, enjoying the soft feel of it on his aching body. If Claire had returned with the wine, she must have decided to let him soak for a while longer. He pushed open the flimsy plywood door and stepped into darkness.

Claire must still be out, gamely hunting down an off licence. Persistence was another facet of her personality that he both envied and occasionally despised. He crossed to the bed and turned on the bedside lamp, dropping the towel and fishing around on the floor for his jeans. Unable to locate them, he got down on his hands and knees and thrust a hand under the bed.

His fingers made contact with what could only be flesh. Cold flesh.

Breathing heavily, Frank felt the cool skin of an arm, the creased material of a shirt or blouse.

He pulled away his hand.

Slowly, carefully, he bent down near the floor and raised the sheets that hung down the side of the bed, their tip touching the stained carpet. Peering under the bed, he stared into Claire's open eyes. Only then did he allow himself to scream.

VI

Terry sat up in bed, his skin crawling with the sensation of a million ants moving in a wave over his body. He'd heard a scream; he was sure of it. That was what had woken him. Terry listened hard, trying to make out sounds other than the quiet snoring of other patients, the *swoosh-swoosh* of running-shoes on the tiled floor, the hum of the ventilation system.

The scream did not come again. Perhaps he'd dreamt it, dredged it up from some nightmare he'd been having?

He couldn't be sure, but he felt that it had sounded like his mother.

Terry got out of bed and walked out of the ward, passing sleeping children and a nurse engrossed in some late-night quiz show he was watching on a tiny portable television. He moved along the corridor in silence, determined not to wake anyone, or to draw attention to his progress. He didn't know where he was going, but he did know that his family needed him.

After walking the halls for what seemed like a long time Terry stopped, listening to the eerie near-silence. His parents had denied the existence of the boy, Franz, saying that Terry had imagined the other. But he was certain that the boy had been there, and that he meant Terry harm. More than that, he felt that Franz meant to hurt his parents, specifically his dad. The fact that they almost shared a Christian name was not lost on him. It seemed important somehow, as if part of some grand scheme or plan.

Terry continued on his way, seeking an exit. He saw the lifts up ahead, their doors firmly shut. He hurried, knowing that to summon them he'd have to wait around in full view, risking exposure.

He pressed the button to call the lift. The little "up" arrow glowed green; Terry waited, feeling tense and anxious. He heard the sound of the lift mechanism hauling the metal box up its grimy shaft: the hum of motors, the clank of machinery. *Come on!* he thought, his leg twitching with impatience.

The lift doors opened a fraction, then stuck with a thin band of black between them. Terry lurched forward and pushed his fingers into the gap, attempting to tug the doors apart. He strained, focusing all of his strength on that thin vertical aperture. Finally, the doors reluctantly began to open.

Franz stood on the other side, dressed in dirty jeans and a torn white T-shirt. His face was smeared with dirt, his eyes like stones pressed into river clay and his mouth was curved into a slow grin. "Going down?" he said, and his voice was like sticks being clashed together: dry, empty. Dead.

Terry ran for the stairs, aware that his feet were bare. He was dressed in hospital-issue pyjamas that had a flap at the rear: his arse was waving in the cold air.

He slammed through the doors and hurled himself into the stairwell, smashing a shoulder into the wall on the way down. The pain didn't bother him; he was more concerned with outrunning Franz. Footsteps padded behind him, possibly a level up from his current position but still too close for comfort.

When he reached the ground floor Terry fully expected to be accosted and led back to the ward, but there was no one around. The hospital was unnaturally empty. Surely there should be night staff wandering the wards, checking up on things? And where were the late-night admissions? This only added to the sense of dreamy inevitability that he was experiencing, and when he stumbled out of the main doors into the parking area, Terry realised that he was all alone.

VII

Frank lay his wife on the bed, holding back tears. She was breathing; her airways were open. He picked up the telephone to call yet another ambulance, but was halted by the sound of her voice: "No. I'm fine."

Frank replaced the receiver in its cradle and returned his attention to the bed. To Claire. "What happened? What the hell is going on?"

"Hang on a second, just until I can get myself focused."

"What the fuck were you doing lying under the bed? I thought you were dead!"

Shadows moved on either side of him, rippling like black fabric. Frank felt like the walls were closing in.

"Under the bed?" her face was blank, the expression one of utter confusion. "I... I thought I saw someone in the car when I got back here with the wine. When I opened the door, there was nobody in there, but then I sort of blacked out. The last thing I remember is being carried into the room."

Frank was beginning to lose his grip; fear clawed at his spine. "So, somebody knocked you out and carried you in here, then hid you under the bed. Is that what you're saying?"

"I don't know what I'm saying, Frank. I haven't a clue what happened. All I know is that I thought I saw a boy in our car, and when I looked inside he wasn't there. Then I woke up here on the bed."

"A boy?"

"Yes, Frank. A boy. A little boy."

"Terry said he saw a boy; that the boy pushed him down that hole into the basement. What did he look like, Claire?"

She sat up, rubbing her head with a shaking hand. Then she looked at him, her eyes focusing on his face. "Tall, skinny. With blonde hair and a weird crooked grin."

She paused, a sudden animation in her face. "My God, Frank. He looked *exactly* like you did when you were a child."

VIII

Terry moved fast, keeping low to the ground where he could and avoiding well-trafficked routes. All he could remember was that his mother had told him the hotel where they were staying was near the river, and that they were registered in room number 17.

It wasn't much, but it was all he had to go on.

He followed the signs for a riverside cycle route, hoping that he would stumble upon the correct place. He was going by instinct, guided by the tenacious bond between mother and son: if he concentrated hard enough, he could sense her out there in the night. And she was in deep trouble.

He kept his eyes dead ahead; whenever he deviated from this, he saw unpleasant sights on *either* side. The boy was pacing him, and whenever Terry looked to the side — either side — he saw the pale willowy figure running level with him, swift as a jungle beast.

He was beginning to change his mind as to whether or not Franz meant him harm. So far the boy had botched two clear chances: back at the site of the old orphanage, and then in the hospital.

It was almost as if Franz was trying to subtly lead him somewhere. Was he herding him away from the hospital? And back at the ruins of Riven Manor, had he pushed Terry into the basement to hide him?

It seemed ludicrous, but the more Terry thought about it the more it made sense. It wasn't the boy who was chasing him, it was something else: something *terrible*.

IX

Frank smoked a cigarette outside the hotel room, standing on the balcony and looking down at the sparkling river. A layer of darkness rippled across the surface of the water, moving like a sheet. There were shapes beneath the sheet, and they were rolling and writhing, like lovers lost in an embrace. Frank watched them squirm, wondering if they were real or if he was in the middle of a mental breakdown.

He threw the ciggy over the balcony and went back into the room.

Claire was taking a shower; he could hear the hiss of water through the thin wood of door. Sometimes he thought how easy it would be to hurt her. He didn't have these thoughts often, but when they came they were intensely unpleasant. These small fictional deaths felt like sacrificial offerings to the bad deeds of his past, imagined atrocities designed to keep the real monsters at bay. Food for the beasts within.

He'd killed her off in his books and stories, of course, making her the victim in fiction that she refused to be in real life. Terry, too: he'd murdered the kid so many times that he no longer felt guilty.

A cold creeping sensation stippled his back, coming through the open balcony door. Cold fingers caressed his shoulder blades, easing out the tension. Those lovers he'd viewed from the balcony had climbed up to pay him a visit. A voice whispered to him, familiar somehow and bringing with it the uneasy recollection of so much fear, so much guilt.

It was a voice Frank had not heard for many years, not since he'd left the orphanage after being fostered by a nice family named the Links from North London. Finally they had legally adopted him, helping rid him of the memories that scarred him like a heavy blade. He'd managed to leave his pain and debasement behind, but now Riven Manor was calling out to him once more, reaching from the gaping ruins to drag him back. For years he'd managed to divert the voice into his writing, but lately it had been too loud, to persistent.

It had begun when he started work on the new book, the most blatantly autobiographical thing he'd ever written. A twisted fairytale featuring the Hugger, a creature who *loved* its victims to death. Like the staff at Riven Manor all those years ago, it used twisted affection to render children senseless. Frank had used what few scattered memories of his time at Riven Manor he could muster to invest the evil with a sense of realism, of verisimilitude. This was no metaphorical monster: not this time. It was the real thing.

Smooth arms enveloped him from behind in an almost liquid motion. And he was unable to shrug off the advances of the thing that wanted to have him one last time.

X

Terry reached the river and realised that he was standing on the wrong side. The hotel stood directly ahead of him, looming on the opposite bank across a black strip of gurgling water. Franz treaded water in the middle of the river, rapidly shaking his head. He wanted Terry to turn back.

Now that he'd worked out that the boy meant him no real harm things had changed. The dynamic had shifted. Instead of fear, Terry felt a sharp pang of curiosity. Who was this boy Franz, and why was he here? And, more importantly, what did he think he was protecting Terry from?

Terry waded into the river, oblivious to the icy waters that rose up his legs and numbed his genitals. It felt like cold fingers grabbing him down there.

"You *were* trying to protect me, weren't you?" he said to the boy in the river.

Franz slowly sunk beneath the black surface of the water, a mournful look on his doughy face. The waters closed over his head like tar, sucking him down into the hungry depths. The last thing Terry saw before the boy vanished was the top of his blonde head.

Terry pushed on, swimming in a doggy-paddle across to the other side. That unpleasant sensation of hands tugging at his crotch did not disappear; if anything, it grew stronger the closer he got to the opposite bank. A wet voice whispered in his ear. He could not make out the words, but they seemed to hold sexual connotations. Some of the phrases that poured into his ear burned his soul like a hot iron, despite him never having heard them before and not being able to fully understand their meaning.

He climbed out on the other side, breathless and terrified. He realised now that there was something here, something that had emerged from the dank interior passages of Riven Manor when the bulldozers had done their work, tearing the place apart.

Whatever negative energy had been compressed between the bricks, or had seeped into the wood and fibres, had been released into the outside world.

XI

"What's wrong with you, Frank?" Claire slid across the bed as she buttoned her blouse, suddenly wary of her husband and needing to place the piece of furniture between them. His face had altered somehow in the last five minutes, as if the skin had slackened on the bone beneath.

He walked to the bottom of the bed, grinning like a fool. His eyes were dead. His lips were thin and compressed, pulled back from his teeth in a silent snarl.

"Frank?"

"Frank isn't here. If you'd like to leave a message, I'm sure he'll get back to you." He giggled, his muscular shoulders twitching.

"Please, honey. What's happening?"

"Where's the boy, pretty Claire? Where's your son, your little Terry? We want to *playyyy* with him."

In that moment Claire realised that, as the thing before her had said, Frank was no longer present in his own body. His personality had been usurped, submerged beneath this... this *monster*.

"He was promised to us a long time ago, back when we used to *playyyy* with your hubby. He was a game boy, little Frank. Such a pretty, soft mouth; such smooth, smooth little hands. We took great pleasure from him, back in the day.

"In the deep dark parts of night, we crept into their little rooms. We took what we wanted, left behind scars that never heal. We were their own most hated nightmares; we were their bestest friends. We were the ones charged with their care, and we abused the privilege to the best of our abilities."

Their followed a hideous cackling laugh, a sound that made her skin itch.

"My son is safe. Somewhere you can't get to him." Claire managed to get her feet under her, and thrust herself up into a standing position on the mattress.

"You can't hide him from us. We're like Rumple-*fucking*-stiltskin. But even if you name us, we'll still take him apart and fill his holes with meat."

Claire felt nauseous; it sickened her soul to hear someone — *her own husband* — talk about Terry like that. Her poor boy. She wanted to run to him now, to take him in her arms and carry him away from all the filth of the world.

"Ah," said the Frank-thing. "A mother's love. There's nothing better to twist, to beat out of shape and defile. A mother's love can be such a beautiful thing to ruin."

"Fuck off," she said, and aimed a kick at Frank's head. Her foot connected; he sat down forcefully on his backside, a comical look of utter confusion on his face. Those self-defence lessons had paid off; she had a kick like a mule.

"Bitch!" he screamed, struggling to his feet.

Claire leapt over him, her knee catching him in the eye. He squealed, scurrying after her with one hand held across his face. She saw blood seeping from between his fingers, and the sight made her heart sing. She was out the door in an instant, slamming it on his free hand. She didn't pause to listen to him scream again; she bolted for the landing, and hurried down the staircase into the waiting night.

XII

Frank fought hard against the figures that held him down, kicking and biting and gouging. But nothing seemed to loosen their grip; they could not be harmed in any way. He kicked out, screaming obscenities, but they pressed down harder on his flailing body. Their hands felt the same as they always had; their fingers knew his body, inside and out. Even now that their hiding place had been demolished, they still wanted to play their dark games.

The irrefutable knowledge that these entities had been here for a very long time came to him with a vision of men dressed in animal skins running across rocky ground, the darkness around them throbbing with intention. The things that now inhabited Frank had been preying on humanity since the very first men told scary stories around a campfire, eyes wide and filled with a thirst for knowledge of the dark, hands gripping fiery torches and making sparking shapes in the air. Riven Manor was the latest in a long line of nests; its essence was merely their current manifestation.

Wherever human evil dwells, thought Frank in a moment of painful clarity, *they* come to feed.

He could see Claire from a great distance, as if he were watching her through a cracked window that was situated miles away from where he was being restrained. He watched her as she fought, and felt a burst of pride when she escaped the clutches of the spirit of Riven Manor.

"Who are you?" he yelled, still uncertain as to the exact nature of the creature he fought.

"We are you," was the reply. "A bit of your own dark world."

XIII

Claire had always kept herself in shape, ever since she'd been attacked at the age of fifteen. Walking through the park from a friend's house late one night, a man had grabbed her from behind. He'd forced his hand up her skirt, clawing between her legs, and thrown her to the ground. Claire had tried to fight him off, but her attacker had been too strong, too heavy to shift. As he'd attempted to penetrate her, she'd been unable to scream: the bastard had forced her own ripped underwear between her lips to keep her quiet.

She had a dog to thank for her rescue. A young girl from a nearby block of flats had taken her German Shepherd into the park to relieve itself, and the inquisitive hound had sensed danger. It had dragged its owner over to the cluster of trees were Claire was in the process of being assaulted, scaring off her surprised attacker.

The man was never caught. Claire bought the dog a brand new collar and a pillow for its bed.

So for the past sixteen years Claire had attended karate lessons in the local civic centre sports hall; and whenever possible she'd gone for brisk runs through the neighbourhood. It kept her sane, and now it had kept her safe. If it were not for the confidence she'd developed through the years of disciplined training, she would not be here now, running to the hospital to save her son from something she could barely even contemplate.

She knew that thing back at the hotel was not her husband, no matter how much it resembled him physically. However impossible it seemed, Frank had been taken over. Possessed.

She couldn't think of anything more ridiculous. Or more terrifying.

IV

Terry cautiously climbed the stairs to room number 17. There had been no one on the front desk when he'd entered the building, so he'd taken it upon himself to go straight to his parents. He ran past rooms with closed doors, feeling as if the entire population of the planet had turned their backs on him. He realised that he had to do this by himself; no otherwise unmentioned hero was going to appear to save them all on the next page. This wasn't like the books he read; it wasn't even like the ones his father wrote. They all had happy endings.

He had not seen Franz since the river crossing, but could sense the boy's chill presence.

He followed Terry at a distance, trailing him like smoke.

The door to his parents' room was open, and a figure lay on the bed.

Terry entered, peering into the gloom.

"Mum," he said, suddenly afraid. "Is that you?"

"Come in, child," said a voice he did not recognise. And when his father sat up on the bed, the door slammed shut behind him.

XV

The boy was sitting on the edge of the kerb, playing with dead leaves in the gutter. His face was pale as flour, and his hair was dark blonde and sticking out at the sides of his head above the ears. When Claire drew level with him, the boy looked up. He was the image of Frank at ten years old: she'd seen too many photographs taken at the orphanage and then later at the home of his adopted family not to recognise that battered expression, those sad, broken eyes. The perpetually messy hair.

"Hello," he said, standing. He was tall — like Frank — and his hands were small in comparison to his burly frame.

Such a pretty, soft mouth; such smooth, smooth little hands.

"Hi. What's your name?"

He smiled. It was horrible, like someone who didn't know how;

someone who only knew how to grimace. "My name is Franz."

"Listen, Franz, this is important. Are you the boy I saw in my car? The boy who pushed my son into the basement at Riven Manor?"

At the mention of the name, he visibly folded in on himself, wincing. Claire felt like she'd struck him a blow.

"Please, Franz. My boy is in trouble."

"Go back to the hotel. He went there, looking for you. I tried to stop him… but he wouldn't listen. He ran away from me."

Claire felt her heart turn to stone; her womb crumpled as if a vacuum had appeared somewhere deep inside her.

"It's been waiting for them, the children. Our children. I saved myself before it got to that, but others, like Frank, have blocked it all out. They don't remember what happened to us back there, but I could never, *ever* forget."

The boy held out his hands, palms down, and twisted them to reveal open wounds at the wrist. They had stopped bleeding long ago, but some cuts never close; instead they become mouths through which the mute learn to scream.

"It's so very patient. It knows that eventually they'll all come back, one by one, piece by piece. All it has to do is wait."

Claire ran back towards the hotel, cramp almost crippling her. But no pain, she knew, could equal that caused by the loss of a child.

XVI

"Dad?"

"Terry, you have to leave. Get out of here." Frank suddenly had the upper hand; the sight of his son had given him the strength he needed to break free of the beasts that held him down.

"What's wrong, dad? I have something to tell you. There's this boy—"

"Just fucking go! *Run!*"

Terry began to cry. Slowly, and with little sense of what was happening to his father, he backed up against the closed door, weeping at his father's rage.

Frank felt them regain control. He was finished. He could fight them no longer.

Terry sat on the floor, rendered helpless by sorrow. He had come here to save his family, and all he'd received in return was punishment.

They guided Frank's body off the bed, clumsily propelling him forward across the room. Frank was powerless to resist; he was weak as a kitten, weak as a baby. All he felt were the countless penetrations, the cuts and the beatings, the broom handle rapists taking their fun. Still he could not remember everything, but this little glimpse into the darkness of his past was more than enough to numb him to whatever came next.

Frank moved slowly and jerkily, like the puppet he'd always been, his joints trying so hard not to bend, hands desperate not to curl into solid fists. He reached out those hands to take what had been promised in the darkness so long ago: a new plaything for his old, old friends, something to keep them company in the endless night.

XVII

Terry watched in horror as his father's body sprouted multiple arms, hands waving in the air like black ribbons blown in a stinking wind. Far too many fingers reached for him, grabbing him by the arms, throat, and face. He went down as the blackness flooded in, sinking deeper and deeper into its world. It was like quicksand, pulling him under, dragging him in. When he tried to scream the darkness poured into his mouth like water.

More claw-like fingers plucked at his pyjamas, pulling them off his skinny body. Raking his flesh, looking for ways inside.

"*Please,*" he whispered, and then he could whisper no more. All he could do was scream.

XVIII

Frank gave one last push, concentrating his remaining energy on denying the dark figures their fun. He managed to take control of his mutating body for a single second; and in that time he turned to face the door, knowing instinctively what waited on the other side. He raised his arms and closed his eyes, hanging on as long as he could.

"No!" he yelled, firmly and with no doubt in his own mind. "No you *fucking* don't."

XIX

Claire burst through the door like a fury, hurling her entire body weight on top of the surreal monstrosity that was rearing over her son. All she saw was a mass of arms and legs, a cluster of twitching erect appendages, scores of lolling wet tongues. It was the shape of abuse, a hideous pattern of sexual abhorrence.

She tore into its flesh with hands driven by the passion of motherhood, bit and gouged at its faces, pummelled its seeping organs until they were flayed like skinless sausages. She closed her eyes and promised herself that she would not open them again until this thing was done, the creature dead, scattered in chewed-up pieces on the floor.

It didn't take long to carry out her wish. She killed the animal who tried to rape her all those years before; and she destroyed the men who'd twisted her husband so far out of true that he was open to such a hostile invasion; then she mutilated every other deviant who roamed the earth, skulking in small towns and cities, living on cosy suburban streets, preying on the neighbourhood children.

She killed them all. Over and over again.

When she was finished she picked up her son and carried him outside. She set him down on the soft grass and sang him a lullaby, cradling him like she used to do when he was a mere babe in arms. When he fell asleep she took him to the car and laid him gently across the back seat. Then she drove out to Riven Manor, watching the boy called Franz follow close behind, covering the distance in an odd loping run that was more of a gallop.

Franz was waiting for them when they arrived, sitting on a small embankment, not even breathing hard. Ghosts can run forever; they never slacken the pace.

"Frank summoned me," he said as she approached. "He gave me his face and a name very much like his own. I was his invisible friend, the unseen playmate. When they entered his room at night and locked the door behind them, he would call me and we'd go running in the hills, swimming in crystal-clear lakes, climbing the tallest trees in the world to hide from the dark stains below.

"I was his friend. I took him away from it all."

Claire went to the boy and embraced him, her arms passing most of the way through him but halting when he solidified for just an instant. And in that moment she saw Frank as he was before a bit of the dark world had invaded, before his innocence had been snatched away by the very people who were meant to protect it. Nameless. Faceless. Heartless. They'd killed the child and warped the man.

"Thank you," she said; and when she looked into his face it was gone, leaving behind only a slight ripple in the air, the sense of something passing out of view forever.

She returned to the car and unpacked the pieces of Frank she'd transported in the boot, laying them carefully and respectfully on the hardened ground. She buried him there, in the tatters of Riven Manor, hoping that the act would consecrate the earth, laying to rest whatever spirits remained. It was daylight by the time she was finished. The sky was red as blood, and filled with a light that was almost hypnotic in its beauty. She knew that Frank's body would be found eventually, probably when the developers moved in to build new homes over the dismembered carcass of Riven Manor. But she would answer questions when they were asked, cross bridges when she came to them. For now, she was content to comfort her son and keep him safe from further harm.

"Mum?" Terry slipped an arm around her waist and she

thanked the heavens for small mercies: a mother's love, a father's sacrifice, the smile of a little child.

(Dedicated to the memory of Fritz Leiber, Master of the craft)

ABOUT THE AUTHOR

Gary McMahon lives in West Yorkshire with his wife, son and monsters... lots of monsters. His fiction has appeared in magazines and anthologies on both sides of the Atlantic and he is the author of the British Fantasy Award nominated novellas *Rough Cut* and *All Your Gods Are Dead*, a collection of short fiction, *Dirty Prayers* (also nominated for a British Fantasy Award), and the novel *Rain Dogs*. Forthcoming are more stories, and *To Usher the Dead* — a collection of stories featuring the character Thomas Usher, a down-at-heel psychic detective. Recently two of McMahon's stories were reprinted in *The Mammoth Book of Best New Horror* and *The Year's Best Fantasy & Horror*, which pleased the monsters greatly.

STORY NOTES

CHILL

The working title for this collection was Thatcher's Bastards, and I wanted each of the stories to reflect in some way the results of a certain period in modern British history when new monsters were created, or old ones evolved into something different — one of the most terrifying of these, in my opinion at least, is capitalism. This story was written under the influence of the recent "Global Slowdown" in the world economy, and examines some of the fears revealed beneath that particular rock when it was suddenly lifted.

THROUGH THE CRACKS

I saw a picture online that was meant to be a Mid-Eastern Jinn crawling through a crevice in a subterranean cave. The picture was a fake, but the ideas behind it were not. This story examines the fascination we all have with what might lurk between the cracks in reality; and what monsters we might have summoned with our desire to see beyond the mundane.

THE UNSEEN

This one was inspired by reading a story by Mark Lynch, a friend of mine who's also a damn fine writer. His tale featured ghostly beings in York; mine has the ghosts of humanity's dead and stillborn aspirations in Newcastle.

PUMPKIN NIGHT

Because of its confrontational nature, and by way of an armoury of outlandish metaphor, horror stories are well-suited to staring into the mirror of society and reporting back on what is found there. In 2002, in a place called Soham, Cambridgeshire, a school caretaker was arrested for the brutal murder of two ten year-old girls. His live-in girlfriend was accused of covering up evidence of the crime by repeatedly lying about his movements at the time of the deaths — she was eventually jailed for three and a half years for conspiring to pervert the course of justice; he got 40 years for the murders. It seems that the woman's loyalty blinded her to the fact that her lover had committed these terrible acts, and only when she was arrested did she allow herself to confront the reality of what he had done.

OWED

Unchecked consumerism and uncontrollable debt are twin horrors which seem to have first lurched into the limelight during the 1980s; purely modern monsters, these things don't seem to want to go away. I have an idea to turn this story into a novella: the characters keep pestering me, and the Slitten haunt me to the extent that I want to find out exactly what they are and where they came from.

WHY GHOSTS WAIL: A BRIEF MEMOIR

I wrote this on Christmas Eve a few years ago. I was feeling a bit low (I hate Christmas) and was suddenly assaulted by visions of my infant son long after I'm dead and gone. These thoughts bothered me so much that I had to write them out of my head, so I sat at the computer well into the small hours, fighting sleep and feeling better as the story formed on the screen. Not once did I hear the jingling of Santa's sleigh bells outside my window, but I may have heard a single distant scream.

ACCIDENTAL DAMAGE

This one started off with me fooling around and turned into something more serious. I wanted to combine some weird physical creatures with a sort of existential dread, and came up with this idea of the dolls and relics being linked to whatever is preying upon my lead character.

NOWHERE PEOPLE

I think this one speaks for itself. It was inspired by a piece I read in a local newspaper about the murder of an honest immigrant worker trying to make ends meet; a family man who was killed by ignorant thugs simply because he was a foreigner.

FAMILY FISHING

This is another story that began as a bit of a joke but ended up being deadly serious. The issues of family and the traditions we hand down the line to our children have always interested me, and the family name here should, of course, be familiar to every reader of weird fiction.

SOMETHING IN THE WAY

I've tried and tried to remember where this story came from, but cannot recall what specific thoughts triggered it. I think I was looking for a new way to examine a familiar theme, and the title (from a Nirvana song) would not leave me alone. The story came slowly, painfully, but I was pleased with the end result. It's certainly one of my darker pieces, but in this case I feel the bleakness is more than justified.

A STILLNESS IN THE AIR

The title comes from an introduction by Charles L. Grant to one of his Shadows series of short story anthologies, and I guess in that case this one must be for him. I never met the man, but his fiction had a great effect on me at an age when I was looking for something exactly like it. Amid the bangs and crashes of modern horror, Grant's voice remains a constant background whisper: quiet, restrained, yet utterly terrifying.

ONCE A MONTH, EVERY MONTH

Again, this one is about family tradition and the monsters it can create. A lot of the families I know, or have known, seem to hide the suggestion of something dark behind a façade of seeming perfection, and this story is about one such group.

SAVE US ALL

Organised religion is something I've always been dubious about, and this story goes a long way to summing up some of my feelings on the subject. I've never been a big joiner; I prefer to stand at the sidelines, watching, forming my own judgements. The people in this tale are unable to do that for fear of being left behind. I'm sure we've all felt that to some degree.

A BIT OF THE DARK

Fritz Leiber has always been one of my favourite genre writers. I feel smarter when I read his short fiction, and quite often he blows me away with the sheer genius of his storytelling. I was immersed in reading Leiber when I started this story (hence the referential title) and found myself with a day off work and nothing planned to take up my time. So I sat down and challenged myself to a write long multi-viewpoint story: a first draft of at least 7,000 words over the course of a single day. I succeeded in that task, but was left emotionally exhausted. I put away the draft and only returned to it several months later, when I was sufficiently removed from the thing to feel capable of editing it into some kind of sense. So this one is for Mr. Leiber, and I hope that it's not so bad that he turns in his grave.

PUBLISHING CREDITS

ORIGINAL TO THIS COLLECTION
Chill
Through the Cracks
The Unseen
Owed
Accidental Damage
A Stillness in the Air
A Bit of the Dark

PREVIOUSLY PUBLISHED
Pumpkin Night
Estronomicon Halloween Issue (Screaming Dreams, 2007)

Why Ghosts Wail
Bare Bone#8 (2005)

Nowhere People
Supernatural Tales 10 (2006)

Family Fishing
The Black Book of Horror (Mortbury Press, 2007)

Something in the Way
Bare Bone#10 (2007)

Once a Month, Every Month
Doorways Magazine (2008)

Save Us All
Dark Doorways (Prufrock Press, 2006)

THE EVEN
by T.A. MOORE

"In this grim fable, the stakes are suicide by Apocalypse, and the question is what can endure, and what refuses to end."
— *Elaine Cunningham*

In the Even — a city built in the intersection between the real and the not — ruled by the iron whim of the demon Yekum where treachery brewed amidst the ever-changing streets. Ancients dwell in the city who have out-lived their purpose and grown jaded with their immortality. They want only to die and they will take the whole world with them if they have to: suicide by Apocalypse.

Only Faceless Lenith, goddess, cynic and gambler, stands in their way. The fate of the world rests on her shoulders and mankind did not conceive her to be wise.

THE PHANTOM QUEEN AWAKES
edited by MARK S. DENIZ & AMANDA PILLAR

Featuring Katharine Kerr, C.E. Murphy, Elaine Cunningham and Anya Bast.

The Phantom Queen, goddess of death, love and war, returns to strike fear into the hearts of mortals in the anthology, The Phantom Queen Awakes.

Meet a washerwoman on the shores of the river; cleaning the clothes of the soon-to-be-dead; try to bargain with the capricious goddess of war; hear the songs of the dead as they cry for justice; walk with heroes of the past

Revisit the world of the Celts; a land of mystical beauty, avarice, lust and war through stories told by many talented authors.

www.ingramcontent.com/pod-product-compliance
Lightning Source LLC
Chambersburg PA
CBHW050941120626
46552CB00001B/328